Script

L.A. Storm 1

RJ Scott

V.L. Locey

Love Lane Books

Copyright

Script (L.A. Storm, 1)

Copyright © 2023 RJ Scott, Copyright © 2023 V.L. Locey

Cover design by Meredith Russell, Edited by Sue Laybourn

Published by Love Lane Books Limited

ISBN - 9781785646263

Script

Hollywood A-lister Finn might be Canadian, but he needs Cameron to show him how to hockey.

Actor Finn Kerrigan is at a crossroads. After growing up a soap star, then starring in a hugely successful trilogy of action movies, he's finally given the chance to read a heartfelt and passionate script that could change his life forever. The role would be enough for people to see him as a serious actor, and maybe even win him an award or two (and no, a golden raspberry award for his action movies doesn't count). Once established as a serious actor he's sure he can come out of the closet and finally live his truth. When he lies to get the part of a hockey player on a struggling team, he suddenly has nowhere to hide. He might be Canadian, but the last time he skated he was ten, and no, he doesn't have hockey in his blood. With only a month until filming starts, he about to be exposed, but partnered with a player who's supposed to be giving him tips, he doesn't realize how many of his secrets will come to light. Falling in lust, one heated kiss at a time, is inevitable, but giving Cameron up at the end of the shoot could break his heart.

Cameron Chavkin is the face of the LA Storm. And the body, and the hair, and the smile. He's at the prime of his career, men and women want to be with him, and he's skating better than he ever has before. His house sits next to a famous rock star's mansion, his garage is filled with expensive cars, and he's even been asked to mentor a once-famous actor in a new hockey movie. Life is pretty sweet. Until the bad boy of hockey meets Finn, a man on the edge with more secrets than Cameron has endorsements. Knowing better than to get involved, Cameron is swept up despite himself, and when it's time to say goodbye to the Storm's most eligible bachelor is finding it hard to follow the script.

Dedication

To my family who accepts me and all my foibles and quirks.
Even the plastic banana in my holster.
VL Locey

Always for my family.
RJ Scott

L.A. STORM #1

SCRIPT

RJ SCOTT &
V.L. LOCEY

Love Lane Books

Chapter 1

Finn

"But you're Canadian." Atlas stared at me in shock. "Wait, Vancouver *is* in Canada, right?" My agent pulled out his cell phone as if he were going to check where in the world my hometown was.

I stopped him. "I am, and it is." Where did he think it was? South of LA?

His shock turned into bewilderment, and he pinched the bridge of his nose. He'd been my agent since the early days when I was a child actor in a soap and was an uncle-type figure who'd watched me grow up. It was Atlas who'd gotten me a lead in the low-budget *Rapid Action* from Byrnes-Rose studios, which, after becoming a surprise hit, had spawned two sequels, *Rapid Start,* and *Rapid Recall,* and made me a lot of money. And him. In all that time I'd never seen him so confused.

He had a raft of clients, and was used to having

things dumped in his lap, but it seemed I'd finally done something way beyond his understanding.

"But you want to read for the lead in a hockey movie?"

"Uh huh."

"And you can't skate."

I closed two of my fingers together. "A little. I skated when I was younger, but then... acting. I mean, I can stay upright. Or at least I could when I was ten."

"But don't all Canadians do the hockey thing? From birth? I mean, I've seen videos of teeny tiny *Canadian* babies skating around with those penguin trainer things."

I sighed. "Not every Canadian is into hockey, just like not *every* American is into football."

Atlas inhaled sharply. "Blasphemy!" And for a moment he waved in front of him as if he were making the sign of a cross—I'd insulted him and the rest of the U.S. in some way. I enjoyed watching football highlights—mostly because of the men in tight pants— but being picked up to star in a soap at ten meant my formative years had been all about the role, the marketing, being a public figure, and not anything to do with funny-shaped balls.

Or pucks.

My life had always been way too filled with other things for me to get into sports.

Unless you counted me getting into Roscoe Lewinsky, the tight end for the LA something or other, because I got *into* him, and he *was* tight and just as much in the closet as me.

I snorted a laugh, and Atlas stared at me with a comic-book open mouth and wide eyes, as if I'd lost my damn mind and wasn't paying attention to his meltdown at all.

He pointed at my chest, turning a dark shade of red. "You told me… you said you could do this…"

"No," I began with exaggerated patience. "What I said, when I was drunk, I hasten to add, is that as a Canadian it's my civic duty to be the star of the next Grierson blockbuster featuring the great sport of hockey. That is what I said."

He blinked at me as if I'd ripped the carpet from under him, which I kind of had. Case in point, me being offered the lead of a new hockey movie, *The Cup*, directed by the hottest director in Hollywood, Oscar winning River Grierson. The role of Hayden "Mac" McKenzie was deep, and written in such a beautiful way, it was based on a bestselling autobiography (which I hadn't read, because… reasons). Who knew, it could even be Oscar material unless, of course, a meaningful biopic of someone cool came out at the same time. The role I'd been offered was that of Rowan Campbell. He was the classic misunderstood underdog. The one who takes his struggling disorganized team all the way to the Stanley Cup Final on sheer grit and determination alone. Of course, while also falling in love with a sassy and confident blonde woman and sacrificing that love for his team. Cue dramatic music, dark lighting, and an on-ice reconciliation as I hand my tearful yet feisty lover the cup, then skate around the rink with confidence.

All sounded great on paper.

Apart from one small detail.

I hadn't skated since I was ten, and I didn't watch hockey.

No hockey.

At all.

And according to my agent, I may as well hand in my Canadian card right now.

I flexed my muscles. "If it helps, I love maple syrup, and if I wasn't keeping in shape, I could eat way more poutine."

"But no to the skating."

"Yeah, no."

"Well shit," Atlas muttered as he began to pace his office. "You reassured me... you said... fuck... you signed the goddamned contract."

"Yeah, you've already said that."

He continued to pace, punctuating each step with a curse word. It was a long perimeter to pace, at least twenty-by-twenty, so that was a lot of cursing. I focused on the posters on his wall, from movies featuring his clients, including the *Rapid* films with me front and center, my quirky sidekick at my side. Action movies with snark and banter had been my golden ticket to the big time. From soap opera wannabe to the face of a franchise, I'd risen like cream on milk. Who knew that an archaeologist solving mysteries with the aid of a psychic would get so big? Of course, comparisons to older whip-wielding archaeologists were made, but fuck that, there was no such thing as a new story. Add some spectacular car crashes, and the first in the trilogy grossed a lot, and with me signing up just for a percentage, it made me rich. Not only that, but I was everyone's breakout darling.

And the Oscar goes to Finn Kerrigan for his not-quite-dramatic role in Rapid Loss! Yeah, right. No one got an Oscar for crashing cars and searching for treasure while shirtless.

"Earth to Finn!" Atlas snapped his fingers under my nose, and the hysterical thought of me being handed a golden statue for *Rapid Loss* drifted away. Was Atlas done with his pacing already? When he ruminated, it normally took a while, but he'd apparently come up with a solution quick as anything. Or had I been daydreaming too long?

"You'll never get anywhere by staring out of the window!"

Take that, Mrs. Appleton, sixth grade English. Which one of us was the daydreamer with a career he loves?

Which reminded me—I needed to send my annual charity amount to her and the school. After all, besides the accusations of daydreaming, it was her after-school drama classes that had pulled the actor out of me. Maybe I should add my name to the donation this time, get an auditorium named after me, just to show the residents of Gibson Hills how far I'd come. So far, *despite* their doubts that the kid with verbal diarrhea who couldn't sit still, could ever amount to anything.

Obviously, they knew how far I'd come given that I name checked the town every interview, and my mom was all about giving out bits of information from my childhood, but there was no school auditorium named after me yet.

I should get on with that.

"Jesus, Finn! Are you even listening to me?"

"I'm listening," I lied. I could picture the new addition to the school already. A complete stage set-up where anyone could act in peace, with a designated teacher/director, that was a safe space away from the attentions of school bullies.

"So, you agree," Atlas pushed.

Agree with what? "Yes?" I said, hopeful that this was the right answer.

"Okay. It might cost you, but for now, you taking the part is only a rumor, so it won't hurt your brand when you pull out."

"Sorry? What did you just say?"

"What you agreed to. That we pull you out of the movie."

What? The fuck? No. "Now hang on—"

"You just said—"

"I wasn't listening."

He let out a dramatic sigh. "Finn, you know I love

your need to do this project, but we have a potential *Rapid* 4 in the pipeline."

"I'm not doing *Rapid* 4."

"But it's your franchise," Atlas said. "Ten percent of ticket income, and a thirty-five-million payday—"

Like I needed more money. "No. Anything but *Rapid* 4."

"Well, there's no point in signing contracts on *The Cup* if you can't skate—"

"I doubt the dude who played Aquaman could really breathe underwater," I reminded him.

Atlas closed his eyes, pinched his nose again, tense, frowning, and exasperated. "You can't special effect away the fact that you're not able to fucking skate, Finn."

"I have time. Filming doesn't start until July. So, that's what, six weeks? I'll learn to skate just like I learned how to rappel down a mountain."

Atlas muttered under his breath as I stared at the movie poster for *Rapid 2: Rapid Start*, in which I was seen in the montage as I rappelled heroically to save my sidekick, the bespectacled psychic. I'd cleaned up good on that poster.

At least I think I did. Doubts were my constant companion, because I didn't always see the square-jawed, blond, and blue-eyed action hero, but instead the kid from Gibson Falls with my deep dark secret. Still, the outside packaging was good, if a little airbrushed where they'd gotten rid of my random freckle. My face sold seats, and that was what the *Rapid* series had been—a money maker.

I could sell the lead in a gritty movie like *The Cup*, and I refused to doubt that.

"Listen to yourself, Finn! It was your stuntman who did all the rappelling. All you did was the six-inch hop from a box into that weird superhero landing where you flexed your freaking muscles and made that joke to the camera about rope burn."

Hmmm. He had a point.

"But I *did* learn how to rappel, and that's the main point."

This time his frustration was so real I sat back in my chair.

"Jesus Christ, Finn, you didn't. You had *one* lesson with Jeff the buff and built mountain climber—your description not mine—and then spent the rest of the week with him at your place in the Bahamas, and you know how much it cost you to stop him going to the press on that."

Ahhh, yes, Jeff. Him of the ass, and the huge cock, and the sexy walk.

He'd *certainly* shown me the ropes in more ways than one. What a week, and well worth the two million I'd had to pay to keep him quiet.

I chose not to rise to his comments about Jeff, and instead, focused on the simple answer to the issue.

"Then we'll get a stuntman to do the skating. Simple."

"Did you take your meds today?"

I attempted to act affronted, but he was only asking because... well, because I probably wasn't making logical sense right now with the amount of things I wanted to say.

"Of course, I did."

He stared at me—looking for the lie. But there was one thing I never skipped, and that was my Adderall. All of this unfocused-me was just a result of the overwhelming excitement at the chance of making a movie that mattered. That was my explanation, and I was sticking to it.

Atlas sighed dramatically. "Did you even read the spec?"

"Yep," I lied. All I saw was Grierson's name on a script when I read the first page. Picture my character, sweating, exhausted, staring at a countdown to the end of a quarter, or a period, or whatever, as his uninspired team headed for a loss. I could imagine the expression I would use, exhausted, broken, resentful even, but maybe hopeful even as the clock ticked down. That one page was close to the limit of my acting ability, but shit, I wanted to emote the broken hockey player more than do anything with freaking *Rapid* 4.

"Stay with me, Finn... Finn." This time, Atlas was right up in my face.

I reared back. Curse my squirrel brain, but I *was* staying with him. I was undeniably in the goddamn room right now, but I did pinch my knee to make sure.

I peered back at the posters and the one for *Rapid Recall* which was movie three in the franchise, and noticed someone had missed airbrushing the freckle under my left eye.

Not good art-guys, not good.

I should get on to that.

No wait—I have an agent—Atlas can sort that out.

"They left a freckle on my poster," I informed him. "They either leave all of my freckles or not—we can't have anything in between."

"Stop changing the subject."

"I wasn't. But a freckle is a freckle and—"

"Stay on task Finn."

"Sorry."

"Look, you understand Grierson demands full commitment, immersive—he'll want you to understand the pain of pushing yourself to the limit. He'll want you to freaking live the part and act your heart out."

I waved at the huge images of *Rapid* 1, 2, and 3, plus the much smaller poster for the indie film, *Where the Ladybugs Live*, which made up the full movie resume of Finn Kerrigan, former soap star turned Hollywood star. "I can act."

I can.

Atlas leaned over me and placed his hands on my shoulders, my chest tightening because I really didn't like being hemmed in or trapped. "When I took you on, son, I promised you one thing. Do you remember that?" How was it that he managed to sound sixty, when he was only ten years older than my twenty-seven?

"Um. That you'd only take twenty percent of my money?"

He rolled his eyes. "I promised I'd never lie to you."

"And?" I focused back on his face, shrugging off his hands.

"You know, and I know, that under the action hero is not another layer where an Oscar-worthy character actor lives, Finn. You're at the level you should be at—you're not the type to live and breathe your part and immerse yourself in understanding what makes a character real."

I winced because this was some character assassination.

"It's not a bad thing, okay? You're great at what you do, flashing your abs, looking pretty, leaving the messy stuff to the stuntmen, and it's made you more money than you could spend in a lifetime. But if Grierson thinks there is another layer, then you and me... we know he's wrong."

I listened to the words, but none of what he said meant I couldn't do this movie—if Grierson was willing to take a chance on me in his gritty piece of art, then why shouldn't I believe I could do it?

"I signed the contract; I'll figure the rest out."

"I want you to reconsider *Rapid* 4."

"No."

"You can't skate."

I puffed out my chest. "I'm Canadian, I'll figure it out."

OKAY, SO FIGURING IT OUT WASN'T GOING SO WELL, AND I'd already gone three days into my thirty-five until filming, paralyzed with indecision.

I wrote a list, checked it twice, laughed at my own stupid joke in my huge empty house, and then it hit me.

Like I did with Jeff the mountain climber, all I needed to do was find an expert in skating, in hockey, someone who would sign an NDA, someone who could make me the best goddamn hockey-playing actor in the entire world.

In the thirty-two days left to me.

We had a team near here, the LA something or other, Thunder? Or Lightning? I looked them up, feeling remiss that I didn't even know the name of the local hockey team. The first entry in the search showed LA Storm, so I was close. I knew it was something to do with the weather.

I clicked into an article—the LA Storm were one game away from doing something amazing in the Stanley Cup, which was the cup of all cups in hockey. I may not love hockey as much as my bloodline insisted I should, but even I recall riots in Vancouver after the local team there lost in a cup final. The LA Storm—and what a cool name that was—were fighting the Boston Rebels.

Okay, so I needed to find someone with the Storm team willing to sign an NDA and teach me. Any one of them would do, and I clicked on the fourth thing on the list: Hockey's sexiest players.

Now *this* I could get into.

Number one was some pretty boy out in PA, all flicked hair and flirty eyes. Oh and married to a guy.

Gay.

How did he manage to be gay and play professional sports?

I crossed him off my mental list. That would be way too dangerous, because what if he was attracted to me, and me to him, and then we fucked, and he told my secret, and I lost all the parts, and maybe not even the team behind the *Rapid* franchise would want me.

No one wants a gay action hero. Right?

Second was some kid out of Florida, a rookie who looked as if he wasn't old enough to shave.

Third was an actual LA Player. Interesting.

Cameron Chavkin, twenty-six, single, and whoa… he was all bad boy oozing with brooding sexiness.

"Jesus, look at that ass!" I said to no one. I clicked the link to a recommended video, one from a previous year's run for the Stanley Cup, and fell down a rabbit hole of sexy, exciting men. LA had been knocked out in the second-round last year, and there was a video of the team reactions. I sought Cameron out.

There was one image of him staring up at the big scoreboard over the center of the ice and he was broken. I thought he seemed as if he was going to cry, but not in a weepy way, instead in a manly, stoic I'm-too-tough-to-cry-but-I'll-let-my-eyes-water-up,   kind of way.

His attention was fixed on a replay of a goal hitting the back of the net, in the background the other team was celebrating, and I took note of the narrowing of his gray eyes as this Cameron Chavkin emoted his pain and loss with resigned grief.

This was me.

Well, not me, but the character I was due to play in *The Cup.*

I wanted this Cameron guy to show me how to be like that, how to do *that.*

I channeled my best Liam Neeson monologue voice. "Cameron Chavkin, I don't know who you are. I don't know what you'll say. If you are looking for money, I can tell you I have a lot of money, and a very particular set of skills in persuasion. I will track you down. And I will hire you."

I laughed at my own joke.

And in my empty ten-room house in the hills, with its three pools and the marble Italianate kitchen, no one laughed back.

I was all alone, and I needed to talk to someone who wasn't my agent.

I considered calling my sister, but she was pregnant

with a third nibling, and so over my regular freakouts over a lot of things… so that was a no.

Or Natalie? She was my beard, or I was hers. Either way, we did promo every so often to keep things settled.

But she was filming in Brazil and the last text exchange we had was all about her falling in love with a woman called Chloe, and I couldn't rain on her loved-up parade with my misery.

Maybe I could call Luca Bennetto? He played my sidekick in the *Rapid* films, and he was also one of my few friends in Tinseltown—growing up on a soap set was hard on friendships but he'd followed more or less the same route, albeit ten years before me.

I liked Luca, and he liked me.

So, Luca it was.

I tried his cell, but it went to voicemail, and I didn't have the heart to leave a message as convoluted as what I needed to explain.

So much for talking to anyone.

Suck it up, buttercup.

Chapter 2

Cameron

NOT AGAIN.

Standing at center ice, my eyes on the scoreboard as they showed the game-winning goal for Boston, all my exhausted brain could keep playing on a loop was...

Not again. Our barn was quiet as a tomb save for the few Rebels fans who had made the trip from the east coast to the west. They were loud. They were happy. Our fans? Not so much. And rightfully so. We'd fucked up once more.

My sight flicked from the chaos on the screen over my head to the desolation on the ice. Off in one corner were the Boston Rebels, this year's Cup champs, ebullient, some weeping with joy. And then there was the Storm.

Our goalie Phillipe was still splayed out in his crease, belly down, the grill of his mask resting on the ice, the very image of dejection. A stuffed storm cloud bounced over to me. There were several on the ice now, our fans' way of telling us that we sucked. Which, yeah, we all kind of were feeling that vibe—thanks gang.

My teammates were stunned—shock and grief playing on their faces. Our captain, Charles Zhang, seemed to have shaken off the stupor of a last-minute loss, but we could see right through him.

"Next year, guys," I could hear him saying as he skated to each man on the ice. He moved to Phillipe and got him up on his skates. The man was devastated. We'd all tried so hard for him, knowing his time in the crease was limited. He was thirty-eight now. And this might have been his last chance. Fuck. This sucked, and not in the good way. "Handshakes now."

Fuck. Me. One of the toughest things to do was get in that line and congratulate the other team on achieving *your* goal. But that was what was expected. Hockey players were nothing if not humble good sports. Inside, we all felt like beating ourselves over our heads with our sticks, but on the outside, we were in a conga line of sorts, only there was no joyous dancing. At least on our side.

Credit to the Rebels, they were good sports. Their captain, Xander Holden, took an extra moment with each Storm player, patting them on the shoulder while telling them that they played one hell of a series.

I wasn't so sure about that. His freaking team had taken us down in five games. This last one of the series had been tight, yes, but the previous losses were anything but. We'd won the first game here at home, lost the second in front of our fans, then flown to Boston where they trounced us, and now here losing again… it was just fucking shit on a shit stick at a shit barbecue.

"Hey, man. Congratulations," I said to Austin Rowe, his sweaty face aglow with their well-deserved victory. His cousins—Jamie, Brady, and Tennant—must be super proud. My family would be waiting for me to get home, then the calls would start and every single one of them would be proud of me, but they'd also commiserate. "Great series. We'll get you next year."

And so it went, same sentiments, same words, until we were off the ice. The final kick in the gonads was that Boston was getting the Cup on *our* ice.

The Storm locker room was silent. Men sat on benches, most soaked in sweat, bruised, and injured. Our defensive line looked as if they'd been run through the grinder. Ollie, our most seasoned D-man, had played the last two games with a chipped ankle bone from blocking a shot from Marquis Miller. Jesus, that man had been a thorn in our fucking sides throughout the series. If he didn't win the Conn Smythe, I'd eat my skate blade. Sans condiments. Guess being in love with a prince did things for your scoring. I'd never felt something that strong for any guy or girl, so all I had to bolster me was the love of my family. Which sometimes was more than enough and sometimes not nearly enough.

I whipped my helmet into a cubby, not even sure if it was mine, then sat down to rest. God, I was tired. And sore. And a loser.

Again.

A low murmur moved through the men as the coaching staff entered the locker room.

Our head coach, Weston Hudain, stood tall and proud, his disappointment not evident, although we all knew he was busted up inside. We'd all had so much riding on this series. This was our year. We were sure of it. Boston had the same idea, though, and they worked just that much harder to achieve that goal.

"Okay, men, I know this is rough," Coach said, strolling around the oval room as he did when he was speechifying. "We all worked hard. We all did our best. This year just wasn't our year. We'll come back in the fall and train even harder. This is a life lesson, men. What you take from this experience will shape you into a more dedicated player. It will instill a drive in you that will carry us through next season to the finals. That fire will burn bright. We will lift the Cup next year. I know this." He thumped his chest. The other coaches nodded as he spoke. Coach Huddy gave great speeches. "I've come close so many times. I refuse to give up when the greatest trophy of all trophies is just within reach. I know it stings now, and it will for a while, but we will pick ourselves up, dust ourselves off, and regroup. I thank God every day for giving me a team filled with such professional and driven players. What you all did out there was out-fucking-standing. I mean it. Don't you dare hang your heads. Be proud of how far we came because I know I'm fucking *proud* of each one of you."

Then he made the rounds, shaking each player's sweaty hand, dropping into a crouch to whisper to Phillippe, who I was sure was berating himself for not stopping that final shot, as well as a dozen others. Goalies were a special breed, deep and emotional. That Phil hadn't mangled the pipes with his paddle after missing that shot spoke to just how drained he was, emotionally and physically. I shook Coach's hand, said the right words, but inside I was hollowed out. Like the gourds my grandmother emptied out for bird houses. That was me. Cameron Chavkin, gourd birdhouse.

No one felt like congregating to rehash the loss. It was too fresh. So, we all showered and changed into suits because losers had to look good when they slunk out of the barn like whipped dogs. Press time had been particularly brutal. We all fielded some pretty stupid questions with all the grace we could muster.

How did it feel to lose in the finals again?

Doh, jackass, how do you think it feels?

It sucks. And it hurts. And it makes a man feel like crap.

"Are you okay?" Prez asked as we made our way to our cars, the few fans who weren't pissed having met us at the players' entrance. It was nice to get the love, even if it was strained, and hear them say they were still Storm Riders. One guy even broke out his cell to play "Riders on the Storm" by Snoop Dogg with The Doors, which a large group of our backers had adopted as their song. They had T-shirts and fluffy storm clouds with our signatures on them. Those same gray cloud pillows some of the fans had chucked at us after the loss. Good thing we weren't the LA Bricks. Man, I needed some more Snoop and much louder to drown out the crud in my head.

"Yeah, sure, I'm tight." I replied, giving Prez a weary half-smile. He studied me closely, his head tipping to the side, dark blond hair buzzed tight to his head, thick beard still damp from his shower. "Fuck. I have to shave now." I reached up to finger my facial hair.

"Not a bad idea," he teased. They all rode me about my measly beard. I noted the tiny light of humor in his blue eyes, which helped lift the funk. "You good?"

"Yeah, totally good. Just heading home to make a blanket fort where I plan to stay until locker clean-out day."

That would have to be one big-ass blanket fort. "Sounds good. I'll be in touch."

"Hey, if you're tripping the night fantastic, or whatever that saying is, mind who you take home, okay?"

I nodded. Great, now Prez was riding me about my sex life It wasn't bad enough that my mother, my twin brother, my sister, *and* my grandmother gave me grief about being *"too free with my favors"* as Granny liked to say.

"I'm good."

Prez gave me a nod that said he had doubts. I'd never once brought any trouble to this team in any way, so why everyone worried about my enjoyment of the fruits of my talents, I couldn't say. It wasn't my fault men and women wanted to be with me. Why the hell should I deny myself what they were offering for free on any given night? Starlets, young actors, musicians, directors, award-winning thespians, Hollywood movers and shakers. They all wanted to be seen on the arm of, or ice-side, with a Storm player. That was how the game was played out here in Tinsel Town. Sports stars were as sought after as movie stars.

"I'm good," I repeated, then gave him a bump on his shoulder with the side of my fist. Personals bag over my shoulder, I made my way to my matte-blue Mercedes. I slid behind the wheel, then chucked my bag to the passenger seat, locked the doors, and let my brow drop to the steering wheel. Then, before the tears set in, I shoved the keys into the ignition, cranked over the engine, and made my exit with all due haste. I drove around LA for the longest time, unsure of where to go to burn off the funk sitting on my shoulders.

Prez would advise that we all go home, eat

something, meditate, and then do yoga in the morning. He was a trippy guy at times.

Phillippe would be locked into his place overlooking the ocean, staring into a scrying cup or something as he tried to see where he could have done better in some mystical way.

My first line mates, Vinnie Boucher aka Booch, and Charles, our captain, were probably heading home, bummed as hell, to mope around. At least Charles had someone to commiserate with, given his little brother Michael, or as we called him Zeetoo, lived in another huge house just down from Charles. I knew they weren't super close—their relationship was fractious at best, but at least they'd each have someone close by.

Yeah, sitting at my place alone, my head full of self-recrimination, was not for me. Nope. I was going to work through this crushing defeat with a bed partner or two. I was open to anything.

I turned off Glendale Avenue into the parking lot for Rumpus, one of the hottest LA nightclubs. Openly supportive of queers, the club was a smoky hot mix of gay burlesque, raucous DJs, and cocktails that were pricey but worth the ticket price simply for the array of beautiful people frequenting the place. I handed over the keys to the valet, then after paying the cover charge, I entered the broody club. The interior was dark mahogany and plush carpets. A mind-blowing mix of LA glam and old-time Hollywood glamour.

The bar was packed, as were the tables. A cabaret

show was in full swing on the stage in the corner. I smiled at the redhead on stage. We'd hooked up about a month ago. Such an eager bottom and incredibly nimble. He could put his legs behind his head. Yeah, that had been a fun night. Messy, but fun. A server rushed over, smiling up at me, her eyes inviting.

"Hey, Choral," I said beside her ear. "Can you get me a seat by the stage and a charred pineapple tepache?"

"For you, Cam, I'll do anything." She led me to a tiny table tucked into a corner. "I saw on the sports app that you guys lost. I'm sorry. I get off in an hour if you want someone to console you." Long red nails danced over my chest.

"We'll see," I replied, weighing whether I felt like taking home a beautiful waitress or a beautiful contortionist. Maybe both. I knew Choral was up for more than one in a bed.

"Okay, Cam." She patted my pectoral, then moved through the crowd, her chunky backside popping as she went. I sat down with an exhalation that emptied my lungs. Sometimes it was hard to be on all the time, but that was life in the public eye. I wished more people understood that...

I jumped when someone sat down beside me. Not just a someone. *The fuck?* Finn Kerrigan. Like... *the* Finn Kerrigan. I checked around for a bodyguard, or at least someone who might tell me what he was doing here in this club. His blue eyes sparkled in the glowing red lights as he gazed out over the crowd as the burlesque performers began a fan dance.

"Hello! Hey, so sorry about the losing thing tonight. I was at the game incognito." He pulled a baseball cap off his gold curls, then wagged a rubber nose with fake glasses in my face. "No one knew it was me, which is kind of amazing. I think I might go out like that more often because man, is it a drag when you want to just be, and people are watching you all the time? Oh, cool! That looks good. Can I get one of what he's having? Thanks. Hey, she's pretty. Do you come here a lot? I like the vibes. So anyway, I need someone to coach me on how to do hockey. You interested?"

I gaped, trying my best to keep up with the hurried flow of monolog and not get lost in his big blue eyes. He was even better looking up close than I could have imagined. He had freckles. I'd seen all the *Rapid* films numerous times and did not recall him being freckled in those movies. He was clean-shaven, as opposed to me with my scruffy playoff beard, and I felt awkward for a moment.

That was new.

A tiny bralette landed on his head from the direction of the stage. He laughed brightly as he pulled it off, then showed it to me as if it were a prized trout he'd just wrangled to shore.

"Look at that!" he announced.

"Um, yes, it's nice," I said as I leaned closer to keep our discussion private. Not that anyone could hear with "I Want to be Evil" by Eartha Kitt pouring out of the speakers. He tucked the bralette into the back pocket of his jeans. "How did you find me here?"

"Oh, that was easy," he said as his gaze moved to the busty young woman on stage. Where had the redhead bendy guy gone? "I followed you from the arena. You have a fancy car that really stands out."

Okay, yeah, that was true. I was still confused. "Why is a big movie star following me to a club?" I lifted my drink to my lips. The pineapple taste strong and sweet.

He dipped his gaze, as if he was shy about being caught out, or maybe shy about the movie star label. Who knew?

"I told you already," he leaned to my ear and replied, his gaze still pinned to the striptease taking place right in front of us. You'd think he'd never seen boobs before. Not that they were shabby boobs, oh no, they were big bouncy ones, but still... "She's got the jiggles."

That made me chuckle. Something I thought would not be possible after fucking up our chance of being the champions. Again. Fucking again. The sigh that escaped was far more dramatic than I'd intended.

"Remind me why you said you followed me." I nudged him with my knee under the small round table of dark wood.

He gave me a wide-eyed glance, as if he'd forgotten all about me. Guess he was a boob man. It would be a crying shame if he was only into boobs because I'd never fucked an A-lister before, and he was a hot property in these parts.

"I need someone to teach me to do hockey. You won the Google results! I mean, okay, to be honest, that hot guy in Pennsylvania with the flicked hair would have been my first choice because, well, hot guy with flicked hair."

"What guy?"

He scrunched up his nose. "A player, on skates, super cute, flicked dark hair, married to a coach, has kids, very pretty, like I said."

He thought guys were cute. Maybe he wasn't just a boob man after all, and for some reason, that sent all my blood south. Then I added up all the clues and he could only be talking about one man who was sadly off the market for all of us since hooking up and then marrying his team's defensive coach.

"Madsen-Rowe? Railers?" I suggested, but he stared at me as if I were talking a second language, then shrugged.

"Whatever, I'm not up to flying to the east coast to learn hockey. Then there was another guy in Arizona, looked like a rock star. Tattoos. He did hockey as well, but he was the goalie."

"Colorado Penn."

"Sure, yeah, that was him. I don't mean to offend, but he would have beaten you out because he was totally sexy as hell. I like a bad boy."

Now my radar was fully on board—he liked a bad

boy? From what I recalled about Mr. Finn Kerrigan, he was the action hero big guy with girls on his arm everywhere I saw him. But he was here, in a club, talking to a virtual stranger about men? Should he be doing that? Was he drunk? I peered at him, but apart from talking twenty to the dozen, he seemed fine. Hyper, but fine.

"… but I didn't think he was suitable because he didn't skate."

"Goalies skate," I said, amused now by his nonstop ramble-bramble way of speaking. Was the guy on dope? His pupils weren't wide as if he were stoned, but my gods could he talk.

"Really. Well shit. I could have asked hot rocker goalie then. Could you connect me with him? Do you know Arizona well? "

I blinked at him. "Uhm, yeah, I was born in Scottsdale. It might be hard to follow him home though since, you know, we're in LA and all."

His drink arrived. He gave Choral a fifty, which would cover the cost of the cocktail and then some, before he took a long sip that emptied half the glass.

"True, yeah, that was why I chose you. Closer to home base. This is amazing! I generally don't like citrus drinks because the acid makes my lips tingle."

I glanced around the club. It felt as if I'd stepped into an alternate reality. Finn Kerrigan seemed nothing like the man I'd seen in the movies. He was… bouncy and light, whereas the guy on the screen was stoic and emotionless. Typical action star. Finn, the real Finn, was the opposite of what I expected from movie star Finn.

"So, I'm a little confused still," I confessed as a young couple came over to get Finn to sign their cocktail napkins. I didn't mind being recognized, but he was on a different level and if we weren't careful he'd be mobbed, even in this venue, which was used to the stars. He seemed embarrassed at first, then signed what they offered, pulling down his cap and asking them not to let anyone else know he was here. They agreed with him when he smiled and showed the world his dimples, and then he waved a hand at me.

"This is Cameron Chavkin, the star hockey player for the Los Angeles Typhoon," he exclaimed, his attention moving from his fans to the woman on stage wearing only a G-string and pasties. "Man, how does she swing those so hard and fast and not hit herself in the chin?"

"Storm. I play for the Storm," I clarified as I added my name to the napkin. The fans nodded at me, obviously not sports people, then faded back into the dark corners of the club. "So, Finn, as honored as I am to have had you follow me in a totally stalker way—"

His sapphire gaze flew from the stripper to me. "Oh shit, was I being creepy?" I pinched some air between my fingers. "Shit. Sorry, I didn't mean to be a creeper. I just wanted to talk to you about some work. I know you're not doing hockey now because you lost."

"Thanks for reminding me." I took a loud sip of my drink.

"Ouch, yeah, that must have sucked seeing the other team get all those touchdowns."

I wasn't sure how to reply to that. "Why do you need me to teach you hockey?" A pastie fell to our table. Finn's eyes rounded. "I mean, it's clear you know nothing about the game, despite being Canadian."

His eyes widened. "How do you know that? I'm using my American accent to blend in."

I lifted an eyebrow. Didn't the world know he came from the frozen north, or Vancouver anyway? "Yeah, it slipped a bit," I lied, and he winced, and then rolled his shoulders as if he was getting back into character. "Anyway, why do you need me to teach you hockey?

"Man, those are the bounciest things I have ever seen," he murmured as the other pastie flew to the table next to us.

"Finn?" I called as I tapped his arm.

"Oh yeah, sorry. I get distracted easily." He turned in his chair to face me, those bright eyes now trained on me.

I found I liked having his attention on me. He was so damned pretty. I moved a little to shield him from other people, the same as I'd shield a teammate on the ice—he seemed way too innocent to be out in public like this, on his own. Unless he had a bodyguard. But I couldn't see one, and no one stopped me from getting closer. Was he a big enough actor to need a bodyguard?

I wasn't sure at what level an actor became so big they needed protection. Maybe he had people out there who wanted to hurt him.

I winced as a sudden need to protect surged inside me.

"I've been chosen to star in a River Grierson movie," he said.

"Wow." That was a name everyone on the planet knew. "Congrats."

"Thanks. The only tiny issue is that it's a story about a hockey player and I don't skate. Or know how to play hockey."

"Oh. That is a problem. And you want me to do what, exactly?"

The crowd clapped as the stripper exited stage left.

Finn rolled his head to the stage, then sighed. "Dang it, I wanted to see how her show finished. What did I miss?"

"She gets naked," I filled in. "So, you need me to do what?"

"Coach me. Teach me how to skate and be a hockey player. I know, I know, you were going to say that I'm Canadian, so how can I be so hockey-illiterate?"

"I wasn't—"

"So go on and say it."

"No, actually, I wasn't going to say that again."

"Good." His gaze moved from the stage back to me. "My agent said it enough. So, will you coach me to skate and be a realistic hockey star? It's totally okay that you're a losing hockey player. I'll still pay you the same as if you weren't a loser."

"Do you say those kinds of things on purpose, or do they just fall out of your mouth?" I had to ask. I mean, sure, I have tough skin but ouch man.

"They just fall out. My agent is always putting out fires. He says he should be called Smokey Bear instead of Atlas."

"That I believe," I said, then chuckled, yet again. "Okay, so how much are we talking about here? Since my season is over, loser and all that, I was planning on going home to Arizona to sulk and make my siblings' lives miserable. How will you make it worth my while even though I'm the third choice on your list?"

"Ten thousand dollars a day." Now it was time for my eyes to flare. "No? Not enough?"

"No, it's more than enough I just..." And here I faltered a bit because while I had nothing to do now until training camp opened—I'd not be posing with the Cup as I'd planned—did I want to spend day after day with Finn Kerrigan? "Tell you what," I said as three dancers in red tights and wild purple wigs slithered onto the stage like snakes. Finn was glued to the sight. I tapped his arm. He glanced my way, smiling so widely it stole my breath. Jesus, he was sexy. "I'll do it for ten per day if you agree to donate what you'd pay me to my charity, CC's Club. We supply inner-city LA kids with hockey equipment free of charge. It would mean a lot to the kids."

"Oh okay, sure, we can totally give your pay to that charity. Are you going to get into making movies now that you lost the hockey cup award?"

"Maybe," I answered. "Maybe I just think spending a few weeks with you is much more appealing than chasing my sister around with a gecko."

"Cool. I love those commercials with the gecko! Did you know that geckos aren't really British?"

That one busted me up. Yeah, okay, this was going to be fun. Something that I sorely needed right now. And maybe, if I played my cards right, Finn Kerrigan would end up in my bed before the hockey lessons were over. God knows I needed an ego boost.

Chapter 3

Finn

"You did what?"

Atlas had moved straight from listening to me explain that I had someone to teach me hockey, to yelling, which was never a good sign. He'd yelled at me just the same when I had insisted in taking the part of an elf called Hobart in *Where the Ladybugs Live*, but when the kids' movie made a shit ton of money in box office receipts he agreed that maybe it *had* been a good idea after all.

Of course, it was. I loved the illustrated book, and I wanted to play the part of Hobart-the-magical-Elf ever since my mom had read me it as a bedtime story. My four-year-old self adored it, and in my more fanciful moments as a kid, and I had many, I imagined one day a ladybug would find me and tell me I had magic. Also, that I was destined to save the ladybug children before their house burned down.

It never happened—I wasn't *magic* Hobart—but I still played a fabulous Hobart-the-Elf if I say so myself. Critics called it refreshing.

Well, one of them did.

The one in my home town newspaper.

Circulation—five hundred and seven.

It was filmed during the break between the first and second *Rapid* franchise movies. It paid me, it paid Atlas, and once my agent stopped yelling, it was all good. It was a film my niece and nephew could watch. Even if Henry said he was too old at eight to watch baby films, Lilly was all over it like a rash. My sister told me Lilly wore her ladybug costume everywhere, even to bed, and that must have been insane given the wings and the pokey antennae, not to mention the obligatory face paint.

I'm not sure my sister has forgiven me yet.

"Seriously, Finn, what did you just say?"

"I hired Cameron Chavkin to coach me in hockey."

"Cameron Chavkin."

"Yep, Cameron Chavkin. Tall, sexy as a fiddle, with stormy gray eyes. Plays hockey."

"*The* Cameron Chavkin?" Atlas wheezed, then went so quiet that I held the phone so I could check we still had a connection. His name was still there, so I decided to press ahead.

"Is there more than one Cameron Chavkin? Oh, stupid question because I guess there probably is given statistically that—"

"You hired *the* hockey star Cameron Chavkin to teach you hockey. The same Cameron Chavkin who is all over the media, not only for his team's abysmal loss in the Stanley Cup but also because he sleeps with anything that moves."

Oh. Well, I didn't know the second part, but whatever, love is love and everyone deserves to be happy. If Cameron chose to show that by jumping beds, so be it, as long as everyone was safe and informed. He might be the opposite of my cold and dark love life, but that didn't matter to anyone but Cameron Chavkin himself.

"Jesus H Christ," Atlas added, as if that helped the situation.

"I now have only a few weeks to brush up on my non-existent hockey skills, plus learning the script, which is more dialogue than in all three *Rapid* movies put together, and it was destiny or something that I found out where he was."

"How did you even do that?"

"I followed him from the stadium."

"To a bar."

"A night club, or I don't know what you'd call it, but there were a lot of naked women, and I have this bra thing that I don't know what to do with now."

The noise this time from Atlas' end was somewhere between a growl and a snort, and then he let out a high-pitched whine and I could picture him pacing his room.

"That explains the photos. You know there are photos, right?"

"Of Cameron Chavkin? I know. That's how I found him. He's the third sexiest hockey player right now."

"Not of him. Of you *and* Chavkin together. At the bar. They're on *TMZ*. It's not good. You're looking up at this woman who… jeez… I can't…" He wheezed again, and this time I felt as if maybe he was taking this way too seriously.

"Are you okay?" I asked with caution.

"Am I okay? Am. I. Okay?"

Nope. It seemed he wasn't okay.

"Fuck's sake, Finn. You tell me you stalked a man to a bar, you propositioned him, you were staring at strippers, and fuck me, do you not understand the meaning of keeping your head down? These photos do not align with your clean-cut media persona and your core values."

That didn't make sense. "If I was there in the bar, then I made a conscious decision to be there and *surely* that is the very definition of one of my core values—"

"Not the core values I wrote down for you to adhere to in public. Not the ones that get you parts. I created your character as the slightly less-than-clever-hero type, who does his acting, does it well, doesn't drink, smoke, swear, or touch drugs, and then gives the impression he goes to church on a Sunday with his steady girlfriend who he's categorically *not* sleeping

39

with until their wedding night." He took a deep breath after that insane run-on sentence.

I parsed all the information.

"Well, *that* person sounds kinda boring. I mean, I'm nearly thirty-one and surely the character you're making up would be sleeping with his girlfriend by now."

"That's not the fucking point!"

"And I do fucking swear," I added as an afterthought.

"Do you even want *Ladybug 2*?"

Hope flared inside me. "Wait. What? They're actually making a *Ladybug 2*?"

"With over half a billion in receipts and merchandising on the first one, of course they are. I don't get why, but the kids loved it. They want you for Hobart-the-Elf again, and they'll have the script with you in two months or so, shooting for next year's Christmas release. You want it, then keep your nose clean, otherwise you'll lose that, *and* you'll lose the Grierson movie."

I didn't want to lose the kids' movie I knew I'd love. And the intense hockey story that might take me to the next level in my career as a serious actor, able to come out and be authentic and not be laughed out of the house.

"Okay."

"I got a quick message at the end of a very short meeting with Luca."

"Yeah?" Luca not only shared the headline on the *Rapid* movies as the psychic sidekick, but we shared Atlas as an agent.

"He said, and I quote. 'Sorry dude will call you when back from Machu Picchu'. I assume he's there doing whatever sidekick actors do when they're not filming.

"Sleeping mostly, and he emailed me the same thing." One friend down, and I was definitely running out of people to talk to.

"Finally, we need to issue a statement about these photos, because not only do they show you seemingly fascinated by the naked form of a dancing woman with the perky jiggly... um... breasts... but the way you're staring into Cameron Chavkin's eyes made it look as if..."

"As if?" I prompted, but got the feeling I wouldn't like the answer.

"I'm not spelling it out for you. Look, Finn. I'm doing everything I can to hide your secret, but random visits to stare at strippers, stalking hockey players, then staring at them like you want to eat them, will make sure that people see right through to your life character and see the real you. Do you want to end up like Elias Lake? Do you recall what happened to him?"

Of course, I did, but tried to fluff it off as if I didn't because it was too scary.

"To refresh your memory, Elias Lake was outed by some twinky social media celebrity. *The* Elias Lake.

Outed as being gay. He ended up hiding in some tiny Maine town where he hooked up with a potter and—"

"Harry?"

Atlas snorted. "I'm sorry, but what?"

"The potter. Was it Harry?"

"No, Finn, the potter was a man who makes things with clay." Oh sure, yeah. I knew that. "The point being that he's not been heard from in Hollywood for over two years. Last time he was spotted by anyone it was in some tiny seaside theater. Is that what you want for your future? Do you want to end up performing for free to people who reek of lobster?!"

I didn't want to lose my career over who I loved, or wanted in my bed, not when it hadn't even happened yet. I mean, yes, I'd slept with guys over the years, one-offs, mostly here in LA, people as scared as me to keep their secrets, but I'd never met anyone worth losing my career over.

It hurt to have to hide myself, made me tense even considering that maybe Finn Corrigan, hero of the *Rapid* movies, coming out as gay, might be a positive thing to any kid out there struggling.

But it was the part I'd signed up for and I hadn't known any different; sometimes, I wished I hadn't been a child actor, sometimes I wished I'd had time between my last appearance on that stupid popular kids' show on that stupid popular kids' network and filming for *Rapid* 1.

Maybe I could have grown up properly then.

"What if I don't want to keep it a secret? What if I want to be the real me?"

"Not this again, Finn."

"Well, it's all up inside me and I can't help it," I snapped at him.

"I know. I *know*. But do you love what you do, Finn? Because you could lose everything if you position yourself too far away from the character we created for you to live." Atlas was trying very hard for reassurance laced with patience.

Worry rolled through me, washing away any tentative idea I might have had over the past year or two of coming out. It wasn't like I needed any more movies—hell I had enough money to last me five lifetimes—but I was an actor in my heart and soul, and what if I lost that? What if I couldn't even get a role in a fourth-rate theatre for a bit part because my lies blew up in my face?

I chewed my lip, and Atlas continued his lecture about talking to him first before I did anything stupid, and I tried to listen, but it was just noise and a lot of things he'd said before.

"… agreed?" he finished. "Finn? Do you agree?"

"With what?" I asked. There was no way I was going to be fooled into agreeing to something I hadn't even heard. That was how I ended up eating a gallon of ice cream when I was ten and losing the lot over my teacher at the school nativity.

"Dinner with Natalie Hager, somewhere in the spotlight, somewhere up market. Okay?"

I sighed. He cursed me out.

Natalie was lovely, another one of Atlas' actors, a veteran of daytime soaps like me, and now entrenched into a string of superhero movies. She was gay as well, so it was a mutual thing to be each other's backup, but at the previous public dinner to show how straight we were, she'd admitted she was tired of hiding.

I was tired of hiding.

Only I didn't know how to explain that to anyone, or for it to be in a safe space where what I said wouldn't leak.

"Sure," I said, "text me the details, and I'll pick her up." I'd arrive at the restaurant, step out of my bright yellow Lamborghini, wearing designer stuff, the right watch, my hair would be screen-perfect, and I'd be the faultless *straight* gentleman I needed to be.

The call ended, and I stared at my cell for a few moments, replaying all the highs and lows of a shitty conversation.

The studio wanted *me* for *Ladybug* 2.

I wasn't allowed to tarnish my reputation if I had any hope of making it to a level where my sexuality be damned.

But most of all... had I *really* been staring at Cameron as if I could eat him?

I opened the *TMZ* app, something I avoided doing unless I could help it, scrolled past stories about Tom

Cruise, Cameron Diaz, a soap star in rehab, and a TikTok of Miley Cyrus and a squirrel, and then there I was, fifth one down.

Finn Kerrigan and unknown man in exotic dancer showdown.

"Man? He's not just a man; he's Cameron *freaking* Chavkin," I muttered, then scrolled the story.

According to the journalist, I'd gone from salivating over naked women, straight through to making eyes at Cameron. All while refusing to sign autographs, telling people to leave me alone, and being a diva by ordering champagne they didn't have.

The fuck?

The last line was a kicker. *Sources confirm the anonymous man is Cameron Chavkin, star of the LA Storm, the hockey team that recently lost to the Boston Rebels in the finals. More to follow.*

I checked the photos and winced. Yep, that was definitely me staring up at the stripper, but I'd been staring because I was curious, I mean, how *do* they keep those tassels on? And the girls were so flexible—I wish I was that flexible, but I was all about the muscle needed for parts and less about the bendy bits. Also, I was possibly the single Hollywood holdout who didn't do yoga.

And yep, the second photo was me staring at Cameron. I zoomed in as far as I could to check out my expression because I don't recall staring at him in anything other than a friendly way, but the picture was a little grainy so I zoomed back out.

It was a perfectly innocent photo, and less worrying than the time I'd been caught naked next to the pool in my backyard, by a paparazzi drone flying at three hundred feet. The resulting picture had been good, and it was gratifying that the publication the pap sold it to, had used a ton of pixilation to cover my cock, which was no slouch in the size department.

Well, so said most of social media, anyway.

I opened another tab to check for stories of Cameron sleeping with anything that moved, Atlas' words, not mine—but immediately closed it down. We all deserved our privacy, including Cameron *stud* Chavkin.

Who I was *not* staring at in the club photo, with sex on my mind and heart eyes.

I'm not that easy.

OH SHIT.

I'm *way too* easy.

Cameron was so sexy, that I couldn't help but stare, and I bet the sex in my head was front and center with the hearts in my eyes. I'd arrived at the private rink I'd hired, in my less obvious SUV with the tinted windows, parked up next to a similar SUV with custom plates and headed inside, dragging the bag of what Cameron had said I'd needed to buy. Which was a lot.

He'd sent me the list, as well as a copy of the NDA Atlas had made him sign. It was embarrassing how long I'd stared at his strong signature while spinning stories of how Finn might look with a spiky surname like Chavkin. I could do amazing things with the K in that last name.

And now I was here in a locker room that smelled a little funky, and yes, I was staring at the sex god himself.

"And this is what we call a cup," Cameron explained, and thrust something at me.

"I've played sports, I know what a cup is," I defended as I took it from him, and he rolled his eyes.

"Strip to your underwear and I'll go through what we need to do to get ready."

"Okay, yeah, method acting, I like that."

He was already dressed, but not in LA Storm colors, which I now knew were purple and blue. Instead, he wore a generic black jersey, no name, no number, and mine hanging up, was white. If this was a movie, then he'd be wearing black to indicate that he was bad to the core, but in real life it just made his smoky eyes pop, and his lips seem even more lush.

Of course, me wearing white was all about my purity, and innocence.

Which was diametrically opposite to the lust uncurling inside me.

"Did you hear me?" he asked.

I started, and undressed rapidly down to my jersey boxers, and then held the cup to my groin, staring down at it.

"It's not going to cover your junk by magic," Cameron said, and reached forward to help me. I scrambled away because I was already half hard, and the idea of Cameron anywhere near my dick didn't bear thinking about.

"What do you feel when you put yours on?" I asked instead, and he stared at me.

"I'm sorry?" He frowned.

"Like your motivation in the scene," I expanded.

"My motivation is not letting a one hundred mile an hour puck crush the boys," he said.

"Well obviously, your boys are very nice, and uhm... important." I gestured at his groin, and then sat back in the cubby, knowing damn well my cheeks would be bright red soon. "But I mean, what are you feeling when you put it on."

"Like my cock is way too big to fit in a tiny space?" he deadpanned, then gestured at his groin before making a shape with his hands that I assume was an indication of his unfeasibly large penis.

And there I go, heat in the cheeks, and thoughts fleeing my mind.

"Are you excited?" I blurted.

"About shoving my cock in a jock strap? Not particularly."

"So, it's a necessity, just a stage you go through to get ready, a safety thing. Your excitement for the game, or your focus, doesn't start until…" I left him to fill in the blanks, and for a moment I thought he'd explain. Only he didn't. Instead, he crossed his arms over his chest, and stared down at me.

"Put on the freaking jock strap, Hollywood."

"With you watching?" I asked in shock.

"There's no such thing as modesty in a locker room," he said.

I swallowed as I imagined the entire team in here waving their dicks around and trying to shove them into jock straps.

Great.

Now I was hard.

Chapter 4

Cameron

IT WAS LIKE WATCHING A GIRAFFE ON ROLLER SKATES.

Finn might have been all that on the silver screen—
or maybe it was a stunt double, given the athletic
prowess I was witnessing here—but in reality he was
not a natural-born skater. To be fair, most of us
weren't. I'd been on skates since I was old enough to
walk. As were most of the guys in the league. Ice rats
the lot of us. Obviously Finn had dedicated his time to
school plays and the drama club. Which had paid off
for him. Also, he was kind of cute flailing around, arms
windmilling, feet going this way and that, as he tried to
maintain his stoic action hero persona.

After the tenth time he went to his ass so hard I
winced, I glided over to him, and offered him a hand
up. This time he took it.

"Okay, so I see we have to go back to basics."

"I used to be able to do this," he muttered, angry at himself.

"Then you'll remember it soon enough," I lied. "Can you stand here for a few minutes?" I asked as he fought valiantly to stay on his feet.

"Yep, the standing I have down pat," he replied then promptly went to his ass.

"Okay, why don't you just sit there for a minute. Let me go get something to help you out."

"Do they have any pillows in the storage room?" He eased up off his backside with a grimace, his hand moving back to rub his ass. An ass that was well-toned in those sexy jeans of his.

"I'll look." I gave his blond hair a friendly rub, my fingers gliding through the silky soft strands. "Just take five."

"Take your time," he called as I skated away.

I plodded down the chute, my skate blades sinking into the padding on the floor, until I found the supply room unlocked for some crazy reason. Perhaps Finn had asked for access to it when he had rented the small rink on South Olive Street. It was a cozy rink, not as fitted out as our Storm training facility out in El Segundo, but then again this place didn't have the Storm financial backing.

I found what I was looking for right off. It was hard to miss the big, bright plastic skating aides along the back wall. I'd thought about grabbing some pucks when I'd first arrived, but we were nowhere near puck and stick ready yet. Chuckling to myself, I grabbed a vibrant yellow skate aide, hoisted it to my shoulder, and thunked back to the ice. Finn was where I had left him, sitting with his long legs out in front of him. His eyes flared to the size of two Thanksgiving turkey platters when he saw what I was carrying.

"What the hell is that?" he asked as I plunked the hunk of hard plastic down in front of him. "Is that a gay walker?"

"No, it's a skating aide. This is what we use with kids and teens who are learning to ice skate."

If I hadn't signed an NDA, I would have been sharing the stunned look on Finn's face with the world *just* because it was fucking adorable. Those freckles were the icing on a very attractive Finn cake.

"This is beyond embarrassing," he sighed, the final traces of macho Finn the movie star dropping away.

"We all start here. Up we go." I tugged him to his skates. His feet went in two different directions. He fell into me, his arms thumping down on my shoulders as his legs turned to rubber yet again. "Whoa, okay." I cinched him tight then lifted a bit to get his feet under him. He was a solid man, lots of power in his well-conditioned frame, but with not an iota of skating skill anywhere in his muscular form. We'd find that though. Hopefully. Maybe in time for him to make his movie. *Maybe.* "Right, we might have to leave the skating aide for a bit."

He smelled good. Cologne and perspiration. A little

sweaty from the past half hour of exertion but that was a smell I didn't mind at all. It made me think of other things that might make him sweat, and my dick started to swell in my briefs. Which was uncool because the guy was as straight as a ruler. With a gentle motion I got some space between his groin and mine. "Let's start with the basics. Standing. Balancing on skates is not like standing in sneakers."

"Yeah, my ass has already figured that out," he said with a sizeable amount of humor. That would serve him well. He had a lot to learn and limited time.

"It's one of the first lessons we learn. Next time when you fall get your hands in front of you, bend your knees, and direct your body to the side. That will save your ass from the pounding it's been taking."

Bright blue eyes met mine. I saw some shock in his gaze but also something more...

"Ass poundings," he mumbled then wobbled.

"Get your arms up into a T position." I lifted his arms as he huffed in concentration. "Good. See now, that's better. Good. So, I'm going to let go."

"Can you not do that?" He glanced down at his skates then at me.

"I'll be right here," I assured him as I released his biceps—nice thick ones I had noted—and moved away a few inches. His jaw clenched as he swung his arms back and forth to find his center of gravity. "Nice. You're getting it. Try to stay in proper alignment." His sleek eyebrow quirked. "I know it's a lot, but you need to know all of this. So, knees over the toes, shoulders back, chest out, eyes forward." His sight flew from his skates to me. I gave him my best smile, the one that generally got me a bed partner, and he returned it with a nervous twitch of his lips before falling down. At least this time he did get his knees bent, saving his ass from another meet-and-greet with the ice. "You'll get there."

He nodded as we got him back to his feet, but I did see a bit of doubt in his pretty sapphire eyes.

By the end of our ninety minutes Finn had mastered standing. I congratulated him then gave him a sticker of a smiling puck that I slapped onto his sweater above his heart. He was not amused.

"Do you give those to the kids in your club?" he asked as I helped him over the edge. In pure Hollywood fashion he draped himself dramatically over the home bench then kissed it. "Oh, this bench is amazing. I love this bench."

"I'd not be pressing my lips to it," I tossed out then realized that I'd put my lips directly to assholes numerous times so maybe I should shut up with the sarcasm. "But I get the sentiment."

Finn was utterly beaten when he righted himself. He was sweaty—still smelling of that unique Finn aroma plus expensive sandalwood cologne—but all the excitement for this adventure had faded fast.

"It looks so much easier than it is," he confessed while I untied my skates.

"That's what most people say," I commented, sitting back to gaze at the movie star.

His golden locks were lank and wet, his cheeks flushed from exertion, making his freckles more pronounced, and his lips were chapped from the cold air. Overall, he was fucking edible. And straight. Straight as Sister Evangelina's spine. I shuddered at the memory of elementary school. Man, those sisters were strict. "You'll get there. You know how to stand now."

"And fall. Don't forget that. I should have a doctorate in falling by the end of this first week," he muttered. I laughed. His downcast expression lifted as he glanced at me. "You have a really nice laugh."

"Thanks. My mom says I laugh just like my dad." His gaze held mine for a long, long time. "Are you doing anything after we're done here?" I asked before my brain could pull it back. "Like, we could do lunch or something. I don't have anything pressing until after our practice tomorrow when we have locker clean-out and that sucks so…"

He pulled off one of his brand-new Bauer skates then sat back, leaving the other still tied.

"Why do you have to clean out your lockers when you'll just be using them again in a few months?"

I shrugged. "It's kind of a thing in hockey. We clean out our stuff, do exit interviews, hang out for a bit at the arena. You know. The one you followed me from." He blushed—it was hella cute. "Anyway, it signals the end of the season. Like when you were in high school, and you emptied your locker out because you were moving onto a higher grade."

"Oh, okay. I never went to public schools. I had tutors on the set."

Oh right. He had been a child star growing up on a soap. "That must have been…" I was going to say cool but all the stories I'd read from other child stars had made it sound anything but cool.

"It was terrible, to be honest, but thankfully there were some kids my age in the cast so at least I had someone to play with. I'd have rather gone to a real school though. I bet you were one of the most popular kids in school being a jock and so handsome and all."

My brain skidded into the boards. *Handsome?* Did this supposedly straight guy just call me handsome? That was not the kind of thing a straight dude said out loud. I chose to let it drift by as a Finn thing. He seemed to be the kind to say cute but wholly unconventional shit. Maybe he was trained to see beauty in other people being in Hollywood for so long. Not that I was saying I was beautiful but… you know, I was okay to look at. I wasn't a troll. My bed wasn't empty often.

"Well, yeah, I was pretty popular. I was a jock though, so that helped. As for school itself I wasn't a fan until I went to college. My siblings and I went to Catholic school so there were lots of rules to follow, things that didn't sit right with me when I began to figure out that I liked guys as much as girls. I got a good education and all, but my mother was always being called in to speak to Mother Superior about my attitude and unholy diatribes."

"Wow, I've never really had a nun mad at me. Did you get in trouble?"

"Nah, nothing like that. Unless you count the shit that I got from my parents when I got into it with the sisters. To be honest, I think a lightning bolt from heaven would be less painful than the chewing out that my folks laid on me." His laugh was soft. A sound I found to be pleasant to the nth. What was also pleasant was that he didn't bat a lash when I told him I was bisexual. "If you're not running off to be a star maybe we could do lunch? I know a great hot dog stand a few blocks over where they make the best Buffalo dogs."

His gaze warmed. Then his phone pinged with an incoming message. He gave me a shy sort of shrug as he rummaged around in the small incidental bag he'd brought.

"It's my agent, Atlas. I have to take it. He might have heard back about reading for Grierson." I nodded as he placed the phone to his ear. Trying to be polite, I slid out to the ice in my sneakers, grabbed the skating aide, and carried it back to the storage room while Finn had a chat with his agent. When I returned to the ice, he had his shoes on and was coming down the chute to find me. "Hey, Atlas has set up a meeting with River, so I have to go do that."

The flair of disappointment in my chest was stupid.

Since when did I care about a cancelled lunch date? Hell, I barely did lunch dates. My grandmother did all the time, but she was in her seventies and went to bed at nine o'clock.

"No hey, go for it." I grinned as if I didn't give two shits because I didn't. Not really.

"Maybe next time? I like hot dogs a lot. I used to be able to eat one in two bites when I was a teenager."

My mind went to a very naughty place. A place where Finn was kneeling in front of me with my cock between those pillow-plump lips of his.

"Cool. Yep, for sure tomorrow. Are you still good for the same bat channel shit?"

"Yeah, totally. I'll be here tomorrow to learn how to stand better."

We high-fived, and I let him get along with his day. And his lunch date with a director who would probably want Finn to suck his dick for a role in the hockey movie. What a jerk that casting director was taking advantage of Finn like that. Maybe I should keep an eye on him in case he—

I ran right into the glass door at the rear exit, my nose crunching into my face as I shook off the impact as well as my train of thought. What kind of moronic bullshit had I been mulling over just now? I exploded out into the warmth of a June LA day, the sun high in the sky, the sound of traffic and a Rasta band performing on the corner floating by. There would be no trailing anyone. That was stupid. I was being stupid.

It was clear that I needed to get laid pronto. A good fuck followed by a rich meal and a cigar would clear my head of Finn Kerrigan's summer-sweet eyes and poor sore ass. Ass poundings. *Yeah man...*

Shit. I reached down to adjust myself on the sly then dove into my car. My phone was in my hand in a flash. Maybe the redhead from the club was free. I began scrolling through my contacts, windows up, heat building inside my Mercedes to the point sweat droplets were running down my temples. I cranked the engine over, cold air blasting me in the face, as I flicked past person after person. I wasn't in the mood for a woman, or a redhead burlesque performer, or the Latino singer at the cabaret. I wanted someone blond and lanky with a killer smile and freckles. No one in my rather long list of past lovers quite fit. Knowing what my dick wanted was Finn but also knowing that was not going to happen, I chucked my phone to the passenger seat, blew out a breath, and cruised to the hot dog stand to buy a Buffalo dog then eat it alone at my place. Music of some sort was echoing from the mansion down the hill, but I couldn't make out much beyond the drum line.

I sat on my patio, feet bared to the gusty Santa Ana winds, as my neighbor Rottie Blade, a heavy metal maven who sang lead in a rock band, tried his best to annoy me with what appeared to be real life *Mario Kart* races around his acreage. What a jackass. I whipped the butt end of my bun in the direction of Rottie's place. It boggled the mind that the homeowner's association had allowed him to move into this quiet and exclusive neighborhood. Money talked, as they say. Money did a lot of things. One thing that money could not do was make a dude like dick.

Looking out over Mandeville Canyon, I sighed out loud. Knowing it wasn't at all what I wanted but seeing no way to get what I desired—or more precisely *who*—I fired off a text to the ginger cabaret performer who was very happy to be free for the night. Thirty minutes later I buzzed him through the ivy-covered adobe fencing that surrounded my two acres.

Sometimes life did not give you what you wanted, be it the championship trophy, or the quirky freckled movie star. Sometimes we had to settle. I did not like settling. Not at all. Which was why I sent the redhead home before he even got through the front door.

Fuck settling. Somehow I would get my hands on the Cup *and* Finn Kerrigan's luscious ass. The trophy I knew how to get. Work harder, train harder, play harder. The man... well, that was a trickier nut to crack.

How *did* one convince a heterosexual macho man to try the peen?

Chapter 5

Finn

RIVER GRIERSON WAS SHORTER IN PERSON, AND ALL around smaller. He reminded me of a meerkat, constantly staring off in different directions, then glancing back at me as if he were guarding something important.

Which he was.

The script for *The Cup* was in his hands and he clutched it to his chest. He was hyper focused as he absorbed the view from the window. He was a private person, no one knew much about him, and some called him weird, others called him eccentric. I called him the answer to all my prayers. Oscar-worthy material in a sports film was hard to come by, but it was unique enough that I could get people talking about me in ways that didn't involve words like beefcake, dumb, or wooden.

The last one hurt—a critic had called my acting in

Rapid Recall wooden, and it freaking bit me in the neck and wouldn't leave me.

Even if the reviewer was right.

The script had been shit—a rehash of *Rapid* 1—the entire thing was made for money. Boy did it make money. Only there were only so many ways I could say things like "Get down! Get down!" or "who the fuck is shooting at us"? or "I promise if we take that ancient cursed artifact, ghosts won't chase us.". I mean, it hadn't been an inspiring script at all, and I was committed to improving my art, I have an acting coach who followed me up from my soap years, but the reviews had reflected my lack of dialogue and the lazy use of special effects and random jump scares involving skeletons falling on the leads, to further the plot.

In fact, Frankie Culpo the sidekick got way better lines, the serious nerd in touch with the afterlife, who spent the entire first third of *Rapid Recall* encouraging my character not to wake the ghosts.

Which of course my character did, without listening to said psychic sidekick—and try saying that three times in a row—and because, that was how shit the story was.

I should say something to River Grierson director-extraordinaire, right? Maybe he was doing the meerkat thing because he was waiting for me to speak.

"So, umm, you called me to attend a meeting about the part?

His gaze snapped back at me so fast it startled me.

"Yep," he offered, but the grip on the script didn't ease, and he didn't expand on the answer.

I was about to suggest he let go of the script and let me read a few lines, but the words died in my throat when he glared at me.

"I don't like the *Rapid* films," he blurted.

You and many others. "Okay?" Why was I here then? Was this some kind of setup? Had someone decided to show me the slim chance of getting this part only to laugh in my face? Heat bloomed inside me, a mix of embarrassment and anger.

"You're wasted in those," he added. Which sounded a bit better than implying me in the *Rapid* films was a crap idea.

"Okay?" Oh my god, is that all I'm going to say? "Thank you," I added with caution because I thought he was giving me a compliment.

"Hmm," he murmured and nodded. "Do you recall when Tony was kidnapped by aliens?"

I blinked at him, not quite putting things in order to make sense of that, until it hit me. He meant the character I played in the *Angel Cove* soap for fifteen years, Tony, who indeed was kidnapped by aliens. Twice. Although one of those times it was his evil twin brother—also played by me—who was spirited away, never to return.

"In *Angel Cove*?"

"Yes. Yes," He nodded, and the grip on his script eased and his knuckles weren't so white. "I was ten

63

when I started watching that, the same episode where you turned up as the heir to the family fortune who was actually the twin disguised as the original heir who he'd kidnapped. You were ten then as well."

"I was." I'd had no idea what I'd been doing when I was ten, plucked from obscurity after winning a local talent show in which I did some breakdancing before launching into a scene from the *Twilight* movie.

"We grew up together, me and Tony."

I smiled at him, and he winced, so I dropped the smile for being one hundred percent serious. "So did I." I started *Angel Cove* aged ten, left at twenty-five, was in *Rapid* 1 at twenty-six, and now heading for thirty-one I'd never really known life away from the camera.

"So, you remember the alien thing?"

"For me or my evil twin?"

"Both."

"Yes, I remember."

"I liked that." He slipped into silence and then smoothed out the script on his desk, the big *confidential* on the front along with much smaller writing I couldn't see, faced me. "So, I saw something in you, when you were standing in the backyard and you did that whole monologue about your heart being destroyed by knowing you'd never find love like the one you did with the alien, Sapphire-Ray. It was seminal. A moment on camera that I can't forget. I mean, I was high when I watched it the first time, but it made me cry."

I blushed then. Yes, it might not make sense for a daytime soap to have an alien romance in it, but then daytime soaps never professed to be high art, and they often ran out of ideas.

"Thank you."

"And that's why I want you to read for the part, because I think if you can bring that emotion to this script then you'll be amazing."

A PA came in with herbal tea and a plate of vegan cookies (or so the little flag stuck into one explained). Said cookies were not on my approved diet list, but I took one anyway, and nibbled at the edge. I'd make up for the taste of whatever the hell this was—cardboard —later in the gym. Or not. Hell, I still ached everywhere from the skate this morning, and I could imagine that when I woke up tomorrow I'd be one messed-up dude. Shame I was only messed up and achy from hockey, when I'd rather be messed up and achy because Cameron bent me over the back of a sofa and pegged my—

"So, it's the last game of seven," River interrupted my fantasy.

I focused on what he was saying. "Okay."

"You're thirty seconds from the final buzzer. You've put everything into the team, you've led them from adversity at the beginning of the year, and the score is tied at three goals each. You have the puck, you ache, your chest is hurting, you're gassed, and you have a broken ankle."

"A broken ankle."

"It's okay; it's taped up."

"That's good," I said, because he seemed to expect an answer.

"So, you shoot the puck. Imagine it in slow motion." He made a square of his hands as if he were checking through a viewfinder. "The crowd is a blur, sweat trickles down your face, the pain is insane, and you have the puck on your stick, and you shoot." He slid his fingers to one side and then back. "We don't follow the puck, we follow your expression, and there's a montage of failure in your head, and then the puck—BANG!"

I jumped in my seat.

"BANG! It hits the metal and ricochets away from the net minder, and you've lost. In the last few seconds you've lost, and it's on you. You're the captain, you're the star, the weight of it all is on you."

I was tearing up, lost in his words, and shit, this poor captain with his missed shot.

"Now read this to yourself and then I want to see you act this out with that emotion you conveyed over losing your alien lover."

I read the scene over; there were no words, just action. Falling to the ice, leaning against the wall, broken, surveying the winner's celebrations and then unable to stare at the score.

I recalled Cameron's expression at his loss, the quiet devastation, the hopelessness, the pain, and on instinct I stood and pushed the chair to one side. I recalled losing Sapphire-Ray in my soap days, I remembered the moment I'd decided to stay in the closet, I pulled the pain and the loss around me like a cloak. And then I fucking acted the shit out of it.

Tears collected in my eyes, unbidden, as I took every ounce of pain I could find and then I slumped to the office floor, staring out at the image in my head of the winners. I brushed away a tear, buried my head in my knees, silent, stoic, then lifted my head and letting a single crystal tear run down my cheek.

River went quiet. It took me a while to come out of the headspace, the feelings inside me so visceral I could imagine Cameron's loss like my own, but when I did, River gestured for me to sit in the chair, and he had tears in his eyes.

"That." He pointed a shaky finger at me. "*That* is what I want. I'll get a contract to your agent immediately."

You will? "Thank you, it's an honor to—"

"Basic SAG-approved fee, but a percentage of takings, I feel like that arrangement keeps my actors motivated."

Hell, it wasn't like I needed money, just the chance to become the actor I wanted to be.

Oscar winner. Free to come out. Free to be me.

"Wonderful."

"Stuntmen will handle most of the skating," he began, and a huge well of relief opened inside me, along with a stab of regret that I might not need to spend time with Cameron. "I mean the hits to the wall and the hip checks, and the hundred mile an hour pucks to the chest, because we don't want our actors unable to act. But obviously there'll be skating from you, action shots, close-ups, and your skating experience will come to the fore there."

Fuck. There went all my relief.

"Sure, I'm just working with a trainer to polish my moves." The first part wasn't a lie. I was working with a trainer, but polishing my moves didn't cover me falling on my ass.

River Grierson smiled then, so wide I thought his face would crack. "I have some final edits on the script, then my PA will furnish you with the final copy, but I'm so happy to have *the* Tony from *Angel Cove* in my next movie."

"Thank you."

"Could you sign this for me?" He passed over a still of me and Sapphire-Ray. God, I was only sixteen in that photo, and on the brink of everything. I looked so young, and skinnier. I signed the corner, and he took it back and held it with as much care as he had the script. Who knew my shitty-ass soap days would get me a role as big as the one I was being offered?

We shook hands, and I backed out of the room as if I was leaving a king, and then nearly stumbled over the PA's desk. She shot me a glance that said she'd seen this a million times. I bet a ton of people fell over after being exposed to River Grierson's genius.

Then I headed out, and shot a message to Atlas about the contract. He sent me a grinning emoji, along with what appeared to be a peach. Plus the words, *you did good. At yoga, talk later.*

And then I headed home, and took the longest bath ever, because that was sure to help with the muscles that were beginning to protest what I'd done to them today, and also, yay, bubbles for success!

WHOEVER SAID SOAKING IN A BATH HELPED WAS A LIAR.

Waking up the next morning was like I'd turned ninety overnight. Even my eyeballs ached, although that could be to do with traumatic crying in River's office. My watch informed me I had only an hour to get to the rink to meet Cameron, and ten minutes of that was me getting dressed and trying not to give in and go back to bed. I dragged my aching ass into the rink a small part of me hoping that maybe Cameron would be busy and needed the morning off.

"Morning," chirpy-sexy-gorgeous Cameron said as he strode into the locker room, wearing purple training shorts and a tight T-shirt. If I wasn't feeling so shaky, I'd swallow my tongue.

"Gah," I managed, and slumped into the cubby, pulling at my T-shirt with weak noodle hands and trying to get it over my head.

"Uh oh," Cameron murmured, and went to a crouch in front of me, his hand on my knee for balance. I wanted him to let go of my knee because, shit, it was sore, but I also wanted him to stay right where he was, crouched between my legs, his bottom lip damp where he'd licked it, his eyes full of compassion. "You okay?"

"I'm ninety-three and clearly arthritic," I whimpered, and he rolled his eyes. "I need to be put down. Find a veterinarian stat."

"Come with me." Cameron stood and extended a hand to help me.

"I can't move. Just leave me here. I'll be okay. Call my parents and let them know I love them."

"Oh my god, what a drama queen." Cameron chuckled and gripped my hands, helping me to stand, and allowing me to lean on him.

I liked leaning on him.

I might stay like this. Leaning on Cameron and inhaling the scent of him and creating little fantasies where he gripped me hard, bent me back, and kissed me.

But no. He had other ideas, shuffling me through a door to an office with a long table and a desk. The table was a low-rent massage space, and when he encouraged me to sit on the edge of it, all I wanted to do was curl up and sleep. He pulled off my T-shirt, eased my pants over my ass and helped me wriggle out of them, plus shoes and socks, then assisted me in lying on my front.

"Where does it hurt the most?" he asked.

Was it wrong to tell him my cock was hurting and that I needed him to start there?

Probably.

"My big toe is okay," I deadpanned.

"Okay, hang on."

He disappeared from my side, and then reappeared with a bottle of oil, and my traitorous cock attempted to get a word in, even if I was lying on it. Oil was good.

Oil was fun.

He rubbed oil into his hands, concentrating so hard a small line appeared between his beautiful eyes, and then he smoothed a hand from my shoulder to the base of my spine, stopping just at the swell of my ass.

Fuck. My. Life.

Was he going to pull down my underwear, start to massage my ass, circles that grew smaller and smaller until he had his fingers inside me.

I groaned, my cock erect and ready to go.

Do not mess with the hockey player. Not everyone wants sex when they see oil.

"Okay. Now relax."

Relax? When my cock was drilling a hole in the thin cover of the table?

So not happening.

Chapter 6

Cameron

WHY DID THIS SCENARIO FEEL SO FAMILIAR?

Oh right. It was the starting scene of about ten thousand gay porn movies.

Originality—zero. Potential to get clocked in the face—one hundred.

But only if I let my hands wander, which I wouldn't because this might be a thing a trainer did for his client.

In porn movies yeah.

I blew off that chastising voice that sounded a lot like my older brother for some bizarre reason. Tax lawyers were so dry, and my big brother Lyle was as dry as a fucking desert. Good thing my baby sister Kelly and I were free spirits. We evened out the priggishness at any family meal with my hockey talk and her discussions of her meditation instruction classes. Mom liked to tease that Lyle had been swapped out in the nursery because no one in our clan was so buttoned-up. Mom and Dad had met at school only ten years old at the time, but they'd stayed friends and eventually went to the same college. Mom was a cosmetic dentist, dad a podiatrist. They doted on us but were waiting with very little patience for someone with their genes to make a baby or two.

Lyle for sure would be first to procreate. Kelly was too young, and I was too... well, too devoted to hockey. That would work as a reason. So yeah, Lyle and his steady girlfriend of seven years, Carmine, would be the baby makers. Maybe he would make little kidlets who resembled the rest of us even if he had been switched at birth.

That was just joshing though because Lyle looked like the rest of us with dark hair and Dad's gray eyes. He even had Mom's chin. So, despite his uptight ways he was a Chavkin, and we loved him.

"Are you okay?" Finn asked, spread out like a holiday buffet.

My mind snapped back from my brother and centered right on that sweet ass covered with dark green cotton briefs—well-fitted briefs at that. Finn was fidgeting, moving his hips as if lying on his stomach was uncomfortable.

"Yep, just warming up the oil," I lied. I was not all right. My dick was in complete control and that was never a good thing. I positioned myself with my erection hidden beneath the table Finn was twitching nervously on.

I rubbed my hands together after applying lots of peppermint-scented oil to warm them then placed my slick palms on Finn's tense shoulders. The aroma of peppermint and abject fear filled the room. Finn tightened even more when my hands landed on his back.

"Christ," I mumbled as I began kneading the rock-hard mass of muscle along his shoulders and up into his hairline. "How did you get so tight up here?"

"Skating with my shoulder muscles?" he replied into the padded tabletop.

Oh-kay. Well, that made no sense but whatever. "Today I want you to try to loosen up a little. Now that you know how to fall—"

"And stand," he added, his voice muffled by the table.

"Right, and stand, you can be less rigid."

Speaking of rigid…

I shifted my boner to the side with a roll of my hips as the heel of my hands worked the knots free. Slowly Finn began to relax. His breathing was still choppy, and his hips twitched, which made my eyes drop to his ass. Actually, they kind of stayed on his ass as my hands just did their own thing and my mind wove raunchy vignettes. Short little flicker movies where I was lapping at the tight globes I was now drooling over.

Finn mumbled something. It was hard to decipher

what as his nose was bent sideways and his lips were pressed to the dark green matting.

"What?" I asked, pulling my wolfish eyes from his backside to gaze down at him. "Are you having a cramp?"

I pulled back, slick hands falling to my side, as he pushed to his hands and knees with haste.

"Cramps, yes, cramps," he blurted as he did a few cat and dog yoga moves, arching his back like a cat then tucking his head and tush inward. "Cramps. So bad."

"Where?" If they were in his calves I knew from years of experience how to work those out. You just—

"Cramps," he replied as he fumbled to get seated while covering his crotch. His hand was in no way big enough to hide the massive hard-on he was sporting. I may have stared at the sight. Finn fell to his side and began apologizing. "I'm sorry. Oh my God, I am so sorry."

There was a wet spot on the front of his briefs. *Holy shit how hot was that?!* My head was now vacant of all thoughts that didn't have to do with his cock in my hand. Or mouth. Or ass. I was vers. All sex was good. Or I could fuck him. I was so down with that.

Excuse me, but this is not professional trainer behavior.

Okay, for starters I am not a professional trainer. I'm a hockey player giving this sexy mother lessons on how to skate for charitable reasons. Fuck off.

Stop being crude and obtuse. Why are you lusting after straight guys? Are you the star of some sad little LGTBQ drama about the gay guy yearning for the straight man? Honestly, Cameron, I should think you would know better than to allow your penis to lead you into this kind of one-sided affair.

Ugh, fucking Lyle. But mental big bro had a point. This was not at all cool of me to be perving on the guy. He was straight. And yes, all guys were capable of popping wood when getting a massage. Didn't mean they were queer in any way. Cocks just had minds of their own.

"Hey, no, man, it's fine. Don't be embarrassed, dicks just do that." There, that should put him at ease. "I know lots of guys who get hard when getting a rubdown. Straight guys on my team. It happens." His bright blue eyes opened. He was still curled into a ball, his hands covering his sizeable junk, and his cheeks scarlet. Poor guy. Someone should help him out. I blinked at the tiny dirty voice in my head. Somewhere in the corners of my brain pan I could hear Lyle choking on the sip of his masala chai then sputtering said tea all over his white dress shirt and checkered tie. Either he was choking on his drink or the demon that ran the lever to my prick had slapped a sleeper hold on him like I used to do when we were younger and still yearned to do at times now.

"I just... this never happens when Tin Pan, my masseuse, comes to my house," he confessed, his voice tighter than his damn shoulders. Which were now drawn up to his ears, so all that hard work was lost because of a stiff dick.

"Maybe she's not as pretty as I am," I joked, hoping it would ease his mind a little.

"She's not," he whispered as his gaze roamed over me. If I flicked my hips right now, I could flip the table over with my enormous boner.

One of those silent but powerful moments took place then. My brain—which was floating in a sea of testosterone—began connecting dots. There were just two. Dot one was that my touch made him hard. Dot two was that he thought I was hot. One two, buckle my shoe, this guy was hiding something about his sexuality.

"I'm incredibly bi," I chanced saying, as if he didn't know that already. "With a new preference for blond men with big pecs, freckles, and a cock that needs some relief."

Oh, dear God, Cameron Mitchell Chavkin, what the hell are you doing here? Why not just hit him with a porn line like, "Why don't you let me take care of that for you?" while you're making a total ass of yourself over this straight man!

Thing is, Bro, I don't think he's as straight as he's playing.

My hunch was proven when Finn, cheeks still candy apple-red, reached out a shaky hand to find one of mine. His fingers slid easily into my hand. His big eyes were fearful but cloudy with lust as he watched me intently.

Bang!

Something clattered outside, and he leaped up as if the room was on fire.

Low voices grew closer—possibly cleaning crew, or admin, or someone else who wasn't aware this was a closed rink situation.

I toppled back as Finn shoved me to get past, catching the edge enough to keep me from taking a total header as he fucking flew off the massage table like Superman.

Panic filled the room as I struggled to get to my feet. Finn was melting down in a major way.

"That did not happen! Oh shit! No, no, no, no, no, nonononononono!" He threw on his shirt, yanked up his pants, and raced out of there. I got to my feet, stepped on the bottle of peppermint oil, and then slid across the room at top speed. The wall stopped the unwanted forward momentum. My nose kissed the chilly cinderblock. Hard.

"Fuck!" I spat, reeling from the impact as blood started dribbling from my nostril, and I yanked up my practice jersey to use as a mop, I held the cloth to my nose, and headed out of the door to find Finn. He was gone. Totally out of sight, so I ran full bore to the front doors. There I caught a glimpse of Finn's car tearing out of the parking lot. Stepping out into the heat I padded over to where he'd been parked and picked up one of his gold and black Prada sneakers, size twelve.

It did not escape me that I looked—and felt—like a

certain prince who had experienced some life-changing moment only to be run out on and left holding a fucking slipper. This one wasn't glass, and it wasn't a slipper, but the comparison could be made just the same.

I had no clue what to do next. My phone alarm reminded me of what was on my agenda next. Locker clean-out day. Like right now. Oh yay.

I carried the slipper—aka Prada sneaker—to my car, dropped it onto the passenger seat, and hauled ass to the barn. Once inside the Cali Natural Gas Arena I bolted to the first men's room I could find to wash up. Face all bloodied was not how I wanted to greet the press and/or my teammates, and I'd already had curious chuckles from security. Staring at my hair I sighed because I'd run oily hands through it, and it was a slicked back mess of waves. So, I doused my head, pulled my fingers through it, and prayed for the best.

Sneaking into the dressing room didn't go well. As soon at the guys saw me they all called my name, shook my hand, and chatted it up. Which was nice, sure, because this was the last we'd be seeing of each other for a few months. Most of the men went home in the off-season. Many to other countries. A few lingered in LA as it was their home, like me, but took vacations, and I would spend several weeks back in Arizona where I had a small condo near my folks' place.

Reporters cornered me near my cubicle, most eying

my wild hair but having the good grace to not mention it.

A tall guy with a thick mustache began the stupid questions.

"How are you feeling now that a few days have passed since you lost?" he asked.

I so wanted to expound on just how shitty I felt.

"Feeling a little better every day," I replied instead, falling back on all the years of being taught to be polite and humble. The hockey players' creed was never be a jerk. All of us puck pushers saw what some professional footballers and baseball players did both on the field and off. Very few hockey players engaged in asinine stunts. Like they say, play stupid games, win stupid prizes. I did not like stupid prizes. So why I'd allowed myself to play that moronic game with Finn and the massage table I had no clue.

I'd been this close to throwing out a cheesy line and wrapping my hand around his cock.

Head back in the interview.

"We're gaining some perspective now on what we did wrong and what we need to work on for next season."

"The defense on this team has taken a lot of hits. Would you like to comment on that?" a female reporter named Lisa asked. She had asked me out once, but I had declined. Dating a reporter was asking to be flame-roasted when things went south.

"Our defense was amazing. I'm not sure why people

are bad-mouthing the defensive core, but we couldn't have asked more from them," I replied with honesty. The D-men had played balls to the wall. We all had. We'd all given up our hearts, souls, and bodies for the Cup.

Every member of the press corps stared at my hair while we talked. No one asked.

Shame my fucking teammates didn't share that courtesy.

Prez ambled over as did Charlie, both eyeballing me as if I had a couple of ferrets wrestling on top of my head. The press had moved on to other players, many gathered around our goalie Phillippe asking him if he was going to retire now. The rest were hovering around Michael—or Zeetoo as we called him on the team given he was Charlie Zhang's little brother—one of our alternate captains. The media was peppering him with questions about why he did this or that. Zeetoo looked like he wanted to punch everyone out, but he'd quickly get over that—he always did.

Prez sat down beside me as I dumped a bag of butterscotch hard candies into my dark purple Storm duffel. Charlie dropped on my left, stole a candy, and unwrapped it. Our captain narrowed his eyes at me, then began sniffing the air like a bloodhound.

"You sucking on a mint, Cam?" Prez asked as he watched the crowd around Phillippe and Zeetoo with a predatory air. Our captain did not like people pushing his men into tight corners by asking personal questions. Particularly when one of them was the little brother he worried about—not on the ice, but *definitely* off the ice.

"No, I stopped on the way to the barn to get a massage," I lied like a rug. It wasn't a complete untruth. There *had* been massage motions taking place. For a few minutes. Christ, I had boned things up with Finn. I had to find a way to fix things, but I had no idea how to do that. I rarely chased people who exited my life. If they chose to go, well, they could go.

"She massaged your head too?" Charlie asked around his hard candy. He was a cute guy, speedy as fuck, one of only a few Asian American players in the league, and this was his fifth year as captain of the Storm.

"Yeah, duh," I snapped, then crammed a Storm hat on my head to hide the evidence of my fuckery.

"I never get a head massage," Charlie lamented then nudged me with his knee. "I'm hosting the end of the season party at my place this year. It's in a few weeks. You'll still be in LA then, right?"

"Yeah, totally." I had made no plans yet. I did have a weekly date with the kids of CC's Club, but I assume since Finn had run from me screaming, that my teaching gig was up, and now I was footloose. Just the way I liked it. Just call me Pinocchio. He of the lack of strings and all that.

It didn't worry me that I wouldn't be seeing Finn again.

Right?

"Cool. Everyone will be there then they'll start flying home. The theme this year is Viking Chic, which is all Little Mikey's idea."

I blinked at Charlie because a) Michael hated being called Little Mikey, and b) Viking what now? Prez huffed about the press way too loud. They were asking our poor goalie some shitty questions, and Prez was hovering ready to beat one of them up from the look of him.

"What the hell is Viking chic?" I asked.

Charlie gave me one of those smiles that made his dimples appear. "Mikey says we need to look it up, Romeo. And please bring someone. That way you won't be flirting with everyone else's dates."

I gasped. As if I ever did that. Please.

It caught my attention that Prez was muscling his way through to Phillippe to break up the endless pokes and jabs at our veteran goaltender from the media, and I readied myself to jump in if things got heated.

Zeetoo on the other hand had gone past being pissed and straight onto arctic temperature calm—just like he did when he was on the ice with the Storm. He had a way of closing down the bad stuff and putting hockey front and center, which I admired. Zeetoo and Charlie might be related, but they were so different—particularly given that they were stepbrothers, and Charlie's darker hair contrasted with Zeetoo who was pale, red-haired, and freckled. Like freckled all over—

because hell, we see everything in the locker room, and I swear Zeetoo is an exhibitionist. Probably because Charlie frowned every time he exposed himself.

"I'll find someone to bring," I reassured him, relaxing as the media left Phillippe alone at last. Probably intimidated by a brooding Prez hovering right next to our poor goalie. "I can't help it if people find me charming and sexy."

Charlie pretend-gagged on his butterscotch then gave my knee a rap with the side of his fist. Staring around at the empty cubicles made me feel shitty. Even though every fiber of my being knew I needed some down time to heal not only my body but my soul, I hated to leave every year, and this year was depressing as we'd come *so* fucking close. Double shitty to be honest. The fiasco with Finn was chewing on me. Somehow I needed to make things right with him, I just had no idea how to go about doing so while still holding onto my pride.

Life wasn't always charming for princes no matter what the fairy tales said.

Chapter 7

Finn

WHAT DID I DO?

What did I do?

One glimpse of Cameron in those training pants, and his erection, knowing he was as turned on as I was, and every single promise I'd made to myself for the sake of career vanished.

I nearly did it.

I nearly reached out and pulled him down on top of me.

Fuck.

The weight of regret was as heavy as the mix of fear and shame I'd carried for so long, and I had to stop the car when my chest got so tight I couldn't breathe. I'd parked in the first place I could find—a vacant lot in front of a boarded-up pizzeria, then stared at the fading signs pronouncing two for one meal deals.

I hadn't had pizza in so long, empty carbs, not

enough protein, had to keep the six-pack, had to stay in shape, had to work hard to be the Finn Kerrigan everyone wanted. I rested my head and hands on the leather steering wheel and groaned.

Stupid. Stupid. Fucking stupid.

But he was there, and he was touching me, and I felt bold and brave, and so freaking horny, and then I'd touched his hand...

I had to get some perspective, consider the scenarios, evaluate the good and the bad.

I could imagine the way Cameron would grip me, then move his hand, and fingers and... shit... it would have been so hot. His expression was beautiful, a want and a need in his stunning gray eyes. And jeez, I was getting hard in an empty lot in my car, and I couldn't do that.

I couldn't desire what he'd done again.

Fuck.

I couldn't even begin to make sense of it all. Cameron could make a ton of money by selling the story of what he thought we might have done, and then I'd lose the Grierson movie role, and then I wouldn't be able to live an authentic life. I wouldn't be able to cross the bridge to being out in Hollywood but still getting work. Actors who fuck everything up before they made it big don't get to cross that bridge.

Would Cameron do that? Did he need money? I pulled out my cell, and typed in *How much is Cameron worth?* It returned a few results for other famous guys called Cameron—I'm an idiot—and I added his last name of Chavkin.

The top hit was a net worth site, twenty-six million.

So maybe he wouldn't out me for money.

But what about notoriety? Would he out me for that? Was I worth more in the public eye than he was? I doubted it—he had years of being an elite sportsman, I had three chewing-gum-for-the-eyes action movies and a kids' movie.

He didn't need people to know what had happened just to make him look good.

I began to feel better. And just to be sure, I pulled down the vanity mirror to check that I didn't appear as if I was losing my shit. As I confronted my stupid-ass reflection, I swore I could see it smirk back at me for giving in.

In that moment I wanted him.

And now I've fucked up.

My resolve to wait for everything had crumbled in the face of Cameron with his sure grip, and his eyes, and his hair, and his thighs, and fuck... where had my self-control vanished to?

I'd nearly traded a hand job for everything I wanted and planned for.

"Fucking idiot!" I snapped at myself, then pushed up the visor so hard I heard a crack. *Great, now I'm breaking my car.*

I sat back in my seat, and settled my breathing, using all kinds of techniques until I relaxed into the seat. It was all going to be okay. I'd go back, talk to him, get him to sign a post-sex NDA, pay him off if I needed to.

I should call Atlas.

And tell him what? Sorry I nearly fucked up; I think my hockey player knows I was more than turned on by a massage. I held his hand. Fuck. You need to fix it for me?

I scrolled the entertainment news searching for my name—waiting for it to pop up.

The first headline I saw was "Secrets revealed derail *Rapid* franchise!"

Heart in my throat I clicked and didn't know whether to laugh or cry. The big secret was that a plot hole had been found in the second movie. I was surprised it had taken people that long to find it.

Nothing about me. About being gay. About me losing my shit over a man I should be avoiding.

Atlas would work it out for me, hide it, make it go away, but he'd make it worse by explaining all other things I'd only just avoided making the press.

My chest tightened as I recalled the warnings Atlas had given, about Me Too, and responsibility and... wait. What if Cameron accused me of inappropriate advances? What if he stated that I grabbed his hand, and he felt like I was using my influence to get him to...

To what?

I don't have influence.

But the media would jump all over it.

Oh shit, oh shit, oh fucking goddamn shit!

I was sweating, hot, freaking terrified.

That was way worse than losing my career—that would ruin me, ruin everything. My family would be dragged into it, I'd end up in the—

A bang scared the living daylights out of me, and after I gasped and clutched my chest dramatically, I side-eyed whoever had knocked there, and saw a cop. I sat upright, years of media training coming to the fore, and lowered the window.

"Is everything okay?" the cop asked me, and it was obvious he recognized me because his eyes widened. "Finn Kerrigan. Right?" he asked, and I was flustered.

"Sorry. Yes, of course. I'm just getting my license and ID." I reached for the paperwork with exaggerated care, and handed it to him, and he gave it a cursory glance.

"Are you aware that you are parked on private property, Mr. Kerrigan?"

I am? I glanced up at the pizzeria sign, then noticed the one beneath it warning of consequences for parking in the space. Shit. Way to add more shit to an already crappy day.

"I wasn't, I'm sorry. I just needed to take a call," I lied, but it seemed to be enough to mollify the cop who nodded and passed back my ID.

He stared at me then peered into the cool interior.

"In the future I'd be careful where you park your limited edition, only ten of a kind, Lamborghini, sir."

"My apologies."

We stared at each other now, and he cocked an eyebrow. "If you could move it on, sir."

"Sure. Sorry." I restarted the engine and smiled my best action hero I'm-a-respectable-citizen smile, then left before things got any worse. Now what?

I'd had my meltdown, was convinced that Cameron was going to accuse me of all kinds of things, and there was only one thing I could do.

Talk to the man himself, but that would have to wait until tomorrow, for our lesson.

If he even turned up to the lesson.

What if he didn't?

I knew where he was right now—at the place I'd stalked him and where the Storm played, doing something with clearing out lockers and giving interviews. I headed in that direction, straight into midday traffic, and got caught up in the snarl of cars and buses around the arena. I did make it to a security line, but I was twenty cars back and as conspicuous as a parrot in a gaggle of geese. So much for getting to wait anywhere near the Cali Natural Gas Arena. A couple of flashy cars headed in the opposite direction, heading away, and when I saw a familiar matte-blue Mercedes, it hit me that the players were leaving and there was Cameron! All I needed to do was follow him again and hope he didn't realize it was me and stop his car to ask me to explain what in god's name I was doing.

Or worse, call the cops from his car, then I'd be in

some kind of weird-ass chase that helicopters would hover over, then I'd end up on the news and...

Stop spiraling.

I stayed a couple of cars behind him as we headed up into the hills, a little confused when he added a convoluted left and right and ended up going around the block with no purpose. Still, I had him in my sights, and there was no way he'd see me when I was blocked by general traffic from his view. At last, we were out of the city and onto a quieter road going up past private gates, scrubby land interspersed with lush greenery, and it was unfortunate that the two cars between us, a Prius, and a Porsche, both turned off, which left my startling yellow Lamborghini right behind his Mercedes. Inconspicuous, not.

He slowed at a gate which opened smoothly, then pulled into the drive as I parked my car half a block down from him.

Now what?

I'd shadowed him home, but now I was on the winding street with views of the valley, and he was inside his place with the gates still open. I couldn't stay here all day. I drummed my fingers on the steering wheel as I thought about what to do next, and then he appeared right there in front of me. His hands on his hips, lips thin, and an eyebrow quirked. A car careened down the hill, a go-kart that looked like something out of a video game with splashy colors of yellow and bright pink, only just missing me and him. The driver yelled a greeting before disappearing around the corner. Cameron gave them the finger as they did, so I'm guessing he knew them. Maybe he should tell them to slow down.

He gestured for me to follow, and then stalked back to the gate and thumbed inside.

I did as I was told, and once he was back in his car, we created a tiny convoy that took us from the gate down a short road to the house at the end.

Nice.

Not a McMansion like mine, but wide and low. Neat, with greenery, and a palm tree, and a brilliant-white front door. I parked behind him, and then settled my breathing, pasted a smile on my face, and then opened my door. This was impetuous, this was idiotic.

I'm so fucking this up.

Atlas will kill me.

Cameron exited his car and came over to me, his arms now crossed over his chest. He'd clearly changed out of his training stuff because he was now in a suit, which had to be hot on a day like today. Also, had they played or something, because his left eye was puffy and there was a cut on the bridge of his nose.

"Are you stalking me, Hollywood?" he asked.

"No!"

"Evidence suggests otherwise."

"I promise I'm—"

"You followed me from the arena."

"Wait. You saw me?"

He glanced at my canary-yellow car. "Difficult to miss."

I grimaced. "Sure, yeah, I'm sorry, but I needed to talk to you."

He relaxed then, his arms uncrossing, and after a sigh, he stalked to the house, opened the door, and waited. Was me going in there just going to compound my situation? What if the media got wind of me holding his hand, while I had an erection, and then stalking him to his home, and going inside? Shit. *Shit.*

"I'm not sure I should go in," I called after him.

"Huh?" He turned to face me, then pointed up at the sun. "I have AC."

"I have this thing…" I began. How to explain? "I don't want you to feel I'm using my influence to force you to invite me in."

He snorted a laugh. "Are you a vampire?"

I was confused, and then gestured up at the same sun. "Evidence says otherwise."

"Then you don't need to worry about crossing my threshold—I invited you in."

"Yes, but…" I pulled out my phone and thumbed to record, pointing it at the ground. "Am I forcing you to invite me in?" I asked.

He glanced at me, then the phone, and frowned. "No, Finn Kerrigan, actor, star of the *Rapid* franchise and a cute film about ladybugs, I, Cameron Chavkin, star center for the LA Storm, am not being intimidated into letting you in my house." He said that all so deadpan, and then disappeared inside, as I stopped recording.

That covered me, right?

After a moment I slunk in after him and found myself in a wide hallway with a wall of photos. This house wasn't sterile like mine; it was filled with images of him and family and friends, along with a couple of hockey sticks laid by a small table. There was even a misshapen bowl for keys painted in bright purple and with the initials *CC* on it. Had he made that? Or was it a niece or a nephew? I had similar things from Henry and Lilly—a lot of things with Hobart-the-elf and ladybugs on—but I hadn't unpacked the boxes they were in yet, because my huge place didn't feel like somewhere I wanted to call home.

Cameron went down a corridor and through a door at the end and I followed, coming into a wide kitchen with light flooding in from huge wraparound windows, through which I could see a pool beyond.

Nope. He *definitely* didn't need my money.

After he tossed me a bottle of ice-cold water, he took a seat at the counter and waited.

Probably for me to say something clever and to explain it all. Emotion welled inside me, all thoughts of getting an NDA fled, and it was the very worst fear that poked me hard.

"I didn't mean to make you do anything," I said. "I'm sorry if I made you feel like you had to hold my hand, or touch me with the oil and stuff, when you were just being good to me because I hurt all over." I lowered myself to one of his stools, thankful they were sturdy enough to hold him, so they should be okay for me. I had more bulk than he did, but he was solid and sleek, and he wasn't a short guy at all. In fact, he was just the right height to—

Stop.

"You didn't make me *do* anything." He sounded confused, and took a swallow of water, which made my insides hot and squirmy. God, his lips were perfect and if they were wrapped around my cock I'd lose it in seconds.

"I did." I lifted my chin. "I held your hand on me."

He stared at me for a while—it seemed like forever —and then he snorted a laugh, which didn't seem appropriate after my admission.

"Do you know Maverick King?" he asked.

I frowned. "Should I?" Was it his lawyer?

"He's six-seven, plays up in Ottawa, built like a brick wall, muscles on muscles, a juggernaut of a D-man."

Oh wait. This Maverick is a hockey player?

"He's a hockey player?"

"That's what I just said."

"I don't know him, sorry."

"Wait." He pulled out his cell and scrolled through the Internet, then turned the screen to me, showing me a photo of a huge man who towered over the skater next to him. "Maverick King, a hundred and ten kilos, like I said, a juggernaut."

"Okay?" I had no idea where this was going but couldn't take my eyes off the way his lips moved as he talked. He was mesmerizing.

"Not even he could *make* me hold your hand," he said, and sat back.

"Oh, wow, is he gay?" I asked, then amended my question. "Or bi, or pan, I mean I wouldn't label."

Cameron rolled his eyes. "No."

"Oh." Then, what was the point of him bringing this man up?

"I don't know if King is queer. He could be. But that's not the point. The point is that even with your movie muscles, *you* couldn't make me do *anything*."

Understanding hit me.

"Oh."

He placed his cell down, then stood and caged me against the counter, leaning in until his lips were close to my ear. "I wanted to hold your hand," he murmured, then before I could do anything but let out a sound that was a mix between *fuck* and *meep*, he stepped back and out of my reach. "Let me show you something."

He walked away, and after I adjusted my pants, I followed him.

Chapter 8

Cameron

THIS RIGHT HERE WAS TROUBLE WITH A CAPITAL F, AND that stood for Finn.

Finn Kerrigan was trouble. He was a closeted gay man who was in no way, shape, or fucking form ready to come out. I avoided that type of situation as if it were an unexploded land mine. People hiding their sexuality were one wrong step away from being blown apart, and not in the good oral sex way. Just look at the uproar over Elias Lake not that long ago. Not that I would expose Finn like Lake had been outed. That had been vicious. But if we continued this, and I had no doubt that we would because here we were continuing it, eventually someone would step off the secret path and KABOOM!

My career would be fine. I'd never hidden my sexuality. I'd not made a banner or waved it around, but I dated who I wished when I wished, always keeping things within the rather narrow and slow-to-adjust rules of the league. The Storm brass, and the league itself, had no concerns over my life off the ice. There were straight players who got into a whole *hell* of a lot more trouble than this queer man ever could.

So yeah, if things went boom, I'd be fine for the most part. Probably, people would think I was something special to snare a catch like Finn Kerrigan. Finn, on the other hand…

I paused outside the door to my gym, debating if I should send Finn home or show him my exercise room. I'd started this trip through my place to make a point about how he wasn't guilty of anything because I was more than strong enough to fend any unwanted advance off. But, as always happened with us, as soon as we were in the same zip code, the drive to pin him down and lick every nook and cranny on his big, strong body took over.

I closed my eyes, attempted to curb the rampaging lust, then blew out a breath before I turned to face him. He was right there. Like, within touching range, wearing an expression that made me weak in the knees. Hunger, uncertainty, and trust all registered in those baby-blues. It was the faith that spun me in circles.

"Do you trust me?" I asked, the question tumbling out unbidden.

He nodded. A simple gesture, a quick bob of the head, but it hit me like a sledgehammer.

"I trust you," he verified, his sight dancing from me to the door. "Is that your bedroom?"

"No, it's my gym." I reached back to fling the door open. He peeked around me. "I work out every day, Finn. I play a contact sport. I have a kickboxing trainer who comes in weekly. There is no way you could force me to touch you. Do you believe me now?"

He drank in the gym, the bench press and the weight bag, the glide board, and the hand weights on a rack, the elliptical, the treadmill, and the stationary bike. After he saw it all, he glanced at me. The uncertainty had disappeared. That was good.

"I believe you."

I reached out to touch him. "Is this okay?"

He didn't move as my fingers found his cheek. I gave his scruffy jaw a caress. Something inside me shifted in a monumental way. This man trusted me with his livelihood by letting me touch him. Yes, I had signed a general NDA, but that was nothing in this equation. Finn had gravitated into my orbit, pulled in like a wandering asteroid. A collision course of heavenly bodies was about to take place. I could feel it in the air—a shimmer of attraction that had us both breathing hard at the mere touch of fingertips to face.

"Do you *want* to hold my hand again?" I asked, my voice raspy with desire.

"Yes," he answered on a whisper, and we laced fingers.

Oh yes, we do have us some trouble in the City of Angels. River City had nothing on what was about to go down here. I tugged him to me, or he came toward me, I wasn't sure, then we came together with no further words spoken, his mouth meeting mine, no telling who initiated the kiss. Both of us had—it was just that simple and possibly catastrophic.

"Can I..." he asked in a soft voice.

"What?"

"Touch you? Can I... can I do that?"

Unable to move for fear of scaring him, I let him guide my right hand to his cock. His big eyes were fearful, but cloudy with lust as he watched me with an intense expression.

"Please." I wasn't beyond begging for this beautiful man to get his hands on me. I wanted to touch him back. He trailed a path to my hip, resting there for a moment, then going that final few inches to caress my harder-than-iron cock. I shuddered, dropped another kiss, tasted him as he pressed against me and we stumbled back to the wall, the only thing holding me up. His touch grew bold, and he unbuttoned my suit pants to get at me.

"Can I touch you back?" I asked.

He nodded. "I need you to touch me," he confessed and that, as they say, was that. I gave his dick a squeeze. He moaned low and long as his cock rocked into mine.

Jolts of pure heat raced through me, settling in my balls as I kissed the ever-loving fuck out of Finn Kerrigan. He was eager for the kisses. His hands were everywhere, pulling at my tie, then shirt, before tangling into my hair. He tasted sweet, as if he'd knocked back a cocoa latte. Since chocolate was not a big part of my diet—athlete and all that—I savored the delightful mix of cocoa, coffee, and Finn.

Somehow, we got our dicks freed. With a grunt, I pushed him away a little, then, as he watched with sleepy hot eyes, I pressed my dick next to his. Pre-cum leaked out of both of us. I thumbed it over our heads, shuddering at the sensation, then began working our cocks.

"Kiss me more," he panted.

And so, I did. With great pleasure, balanced with one hand on the wall while we both began fucking my fist. It was glorious. He wiggled a hand down between us. Two slippery hands felt twice as good. He squeezed. I squeezed. We both panted into each other's mouths. He came first, his fingers wound in my hair, his cock kicking. I followed right behind him, adding my cum into the mix, kissing as I blew apart. He licked into my mouth like a man starved as my dick throbbed.

"So good," he whispered between breaths, his eyes drifting closed as I nibbled at his jaw and ear, our bodies cooling as the chill of the AC seeped into the fading inferno we'd experienced.

"Beyond good," I said hoarsely as I kissed my way

back to his puffy lips. "You want to take this to the bedroom? Fool around some more?"

"I shouldn't. I've already messed up everything."

His words startled me as he began to pull away.

"Nothing is messed up."

"Atlas will kill me."

I stiffened. "Boyfriend?" Fuck. Had I just shared a hand job with a committed man? Wait. Wasn't his sexuality some big secret? He wouldn't have a boyfriend, right?

"Worse than that, he's my agent."

"And he doesn't know you're…" What? I didn't want to assume anything.

"Gay. And he knows. It's a big fucking secret and…" His gaze dropped, and his posture slipped.

"If you go now, we'll have had secret hand jobs; wouldn't you rather leave having had more than that?"

He stared up at me then, his brain working, and his eyes widened.

"Lamb and sheep," he muttered.

"Huh?"

"If I'm going to be killed for stealing a lamb, then why not steal a sheep? Not that the media will kill me." His eyes widened. "They might vilify me though, and then what would happen? I would have to—"

I kissed him quiet.

"Bedroom?" I asked, and that was all I was going to say as I put the ball firmly in his court.

Then, he exploded, and I went along for the ride.

Finn was a wildcat, all nails, and teeth, clawing at my clothes as we tripped and fumbled our way to the master bedroom. We fell through the door, both of us already half naked, his shirt lying outside the gym, mine hanging off the watch on my left hand, the button on the cuff snagged in the band and with a growl I freed myself from the shirt.

The bed was huge. I was a big man who liked room to move, as well as space for anyone who might join me. We fell across the California king, the navy duvet rising as our combined weights pillowed the covering.

"Nice painting," Finn commented out of the blue as I nibbled on his jawline. I picked my head up, turned it to look at the huge oil painting of black gulls flying across a white and blue background, then glanced down at Finn. His eyes were hooded, glazed with want. "I like gulls. Will you fuck me?"

"Is that what you want, baby?"

"God, yes," he replied as he wriggled under me, arching his body off the plush mattress to show me how much he wanted.

"Yeah, I'll fuck you or you can fuck me," I offered, then dipped down to take another taste of his mouth. He moaned into the kiss as his hands began moving over me, pinching my nipples, rubbing my sides.

"Fuck," I growled when he took me in hand. Hips pumping into his fist, I kissed him hard, pulling a series of moans from him as I claimed his mouth. His thumb moved over the head of my dick, smearing pre-cum down the sides, easing the glide just a bit. "I need you naked."

"Yeah, yeah, get me naked," he panted, tugging my dick once more before I went to his side for the briefest of moments. Only long enough to remove his clothes, then throw them to the four corners of my bedroom. The sun shone through the wide, white-framed windows, the white drapes open wide as I liked them, a warm wind rustling the curtains. When I removed his socks, I took a moment to admire him. God, he was cut. Muscles upon muscles. His chest free of hair, his legs thick and strong, his cock standing rigid. The sunlight made his golden hair glow. No wonder people of both sexes desired him. His pink nipples pebbled as the ceiling fan blew over us.

"You are so beautiful," I said as I bent my head to take a pert nipple into my mouth. He yelped in pleasure, grabbing my head to lock my lips in place, then leading my tongue from one nipple to the other. Words that weren't really words fell from his kiss-swollen lips. My hand moved lower, over his smooth belly to his hot, hard dick. He was manscaped down here, a small patch of yellow curls and clean balls. My blood heated. I had to take him in my mouth. Now. I had to tongue him all over. "I want to taste you, baby."

"Yes, yes, taste me." His fingernails scored my scalp, gently, but with enough pressure that I winced. It was perfect. I licked a path from his nipples down to his cock, swallowing him down in a wet slurp that made him cry out. Then, I popped off his dick, pressed his cock to his belly, and took one large ball into my mouth. Finn came unglued as I rolled one orb, then the other, in my mouth, pulling gently on his sac as my fingers searched for his hole. When I found it, I sighed around his sac as I toyed with the furled edges. "Give me... something, God, Cam, I want... need... inside me."

Being a good and conscientious lover, I supported his thick legs, pushed them up and back, and stared right into his eyes.

"Hold your knees," I said, and he rushed to do as bid. Then, I licked a stripe from the tip of his weeping cock to his hole. He gasped as my tongue touched his hole. I licked and teased for what felt like hours, poking at his opening with the tip of my tongue then working a finger into him, spittle smeared over my cheeks, his thighs, and his balls. I worked his ass, finding his prostate as I sucked his balls. He began speaking in tongues, so I removed my finger, gave his hole a loving kiss goodbye, and pushed up to gaze down at him. He was a sight. Eyes glazed with lust, hair mussed, lips puffy. "Keep your knees right there, baby. I'm getting the stuff."

"Yes... Cam... the stuff," he replied breathless, cinching his legs closer to his heaving chest as I reached for the drawer of the nightstand. Inside were a few toys, lube, and condoms. As much as I suddenly wanted to see Finn's hole taking the big dildo in my drawer, I left it for a later time. Was I that sure we'd be hooking up again? Yes. Yes, I was. There was no way on God's green earth that one time was going to be enough for us. We both knew it. "Hurry!"

I smiled down at him. "Eager for my cock?" I enquired, tearing open a condom, then rolling it slowly over my prick. His eyes were riveted to me as I knelt close to his backside.

"Eager for it. So eager," he answered.

I replied by flicking the lid on the lube open and pouring some over his cock and balls. He hissed at the coolness on his hot flesh, then cooed when I ran my fingers over his taint, taking a glob of slick with me, and pressed it inside him. His body was ready for me. My dick was so hard it ached, so I wasted little time toying with his ass. I took myself in hand, tapped his hole with my cock, and pressed in. Slowly, but without stopping, I filled him. He made the most delicious noise when I bottomed out.

"God, you feel so good," I groaned. He gave me a wobbly smile, then clenched. That made me chuckle. "You ready for more?"

"Fuck me so I feel it for weeks," he grunted, his hands squeezing his shins so tight his knuckles were white.

"Anything you want, baby," I promised, and I then set about living up to that vow. Finn took every thrust with a soft cry for more, faster, harder. Soon, I was pumping, balls slapping his rump, sweat coursing down my back, then between my cheeks. "Close…" I ground out, then took his dick in my hand. With a few strokes his body tightened around me as he was coming. Droplets of cum dotted his belly, chest, and even his whiskery chin. My balls contracted at the sight of his release, and my own orgasm hit me hard. I drove in one final time, deep as I could, and filled the condom as Finn watched, his pupils blown, his chest laboring, that cleft chin coated with his own cum.

As soon as I could, I eased out, moving to the side, to catch my breath and take care of the condom. Finn turned to a gelatinous form beside me, his legs falling open after he released them. His arms flopped to his sides, and he turned to face me staring back at him.

"You're pretty amazing," he said, his voice shaky yet.

I wiggled closer, dropped an arm across his damp chest, and slid halfway over him, hungry for more.

"You're pretty amazing too," I whispered, the words feeling more than a little odd on my tongue. Sure, I'd told past lovers they were great, sometimes even when they hadn't been, but this time, it was more than lies. This time… I thought I meant it. He blushed, which was an amazing sight, so I kissed him, then licked up the spunk resting on his chin. It was a little bitter, but wholly Finn, and so I began cleaning it off his body. He sighed and wriggled as I tongued some out of his navel, then went lower. His limp cock began to firm up once I had it in my mouth. His laughter became soft moans of a man who wanted more. As did I. My cock was hard as steel as I rubbed it against the bedding, searching for friction.

Finn rolled against me, levering himself on top, locking his arms to gaze down on me, a soft smile pulling at the corner of his mouth.

"This makes me happy," he confided as he wiggled his legs between mine. His prick lay pressed against my balls and taint, the fat head next to my hole.

"You know what would make me happy?" I asked, and he shook his head. "You inside me. Would you like to fuck me, Finn?"

It took a second or ten for him to respond. "Yeah, I think… yeah."

With that admission, we got to it. I flipped to my belly, forearms on the bed, ass in the air, dick dangling between my legs, and Finn -- bless his soul -- didn't hesitate for a second, even though he'd seemed reluctant at first.

"Do me hard," I said over my shoulder as his latex-covered cock tickled my taint. He squeezed enough lube out of the tube to coat the whole canyon.

"Oops, shit, I think we have a mess," he commented as lube dribbled to the sheets.

"We already had a mess, baby." I wiggled my ass, eager for the pressure of his fat cock stretching me wide. "Now, do me before I change my—" He plunged into me, his dick entering in one long, smooth, mind-melting glide. "Oh *fuck*!"

He leaned over my back, hands on my hips, and

nipped at my shoulder, his weight pressing me flat into the mattress. And there I lay, legs spread out like a frog, as Finn dicked me into the bed. Then across the bed. Then off the bed. The man was a machine. I had to guess that he'd either not fucked anyone in a long-ass time, had never fucked anyone and was going hog wild, or was a fucking beast in bed. Whatever the reason, I was loving the ass-pounding I was getting, even if I were holding my upper half off the floor with quaking arms.

"Finn... fuck... yes!" I shouted when he pegged my prostate with a rolling hip movement that made my elbows fold.

My face met the carpeting, but Finn held onto my hips, thrusting away, until he blew a load into the condom that I could feel. My dick was flopping up and down, leaking all over the throw rug and my belly. As his cock pulsed deep inside me, he jerked me onto the bed, falling to his back with me on top.

"I got you," he reassured me, reaching around to take my cock in one hand as he cupped my balls in the other. "Come all over yourself."

With his breath in my ear, I pumped into his hand three times before I came apart. He rolled me to my back with speed. I cannot say how much it turned me on to have a man in my bed who could match me in strength. A lot of my bed partners were smaller men or women, and most wanted me to top. Not Finn. He gave as good as he got.

When the tremors slowed, I ended up face in the pillow, ass tender as fuck, dick out for the count.

"Oh hell," Finn panted.

I nodded and mumbled something about standing for the next few days. Then he moved, leaving the bed, and so I lifted my head to watch him. He seemed disconcerted, peeling off the condom, tying it, then dropping it into the small can beside the bed. I shifted to my back gingerly. Christ, my poor ass. Not that I was complaining. He began checking around the room, searching for his clothes.

"You don't have to go," I said, pushing up to sit as the sun filled the room with vivid reds and oranges, the breeze through the palms outside helping to cool the room even more. The ceiling fan whirred overhead as he studied me, then the canyon, then the fan over his head. "I mean, you can if you want, obviously, but I have stuff I can make for dinner. We can eat. Maybe... I don't know... watch a movie."

"Not one of mine," he blurted.

"No, okay—"

"And if I stay, I have to know you won't share that I'm here with anyone." He stared at me. "I have to know I can trust you." Behind his words, he was telling me that he didn't trust me, but I imagine he didn't trust very many people at all.

"I won't tell a soul," I murmured.

"And I can't stay long. Atlas would kill me if I..."

"If you what?"

"Took too many chances. If people see me…"

I gestured at my empty house. "Just me," I said, but he frowned, and I knew it was a huge decision for him to stay. "I want you to stay," I confessed for possibly the first time in my adult life.

Chapter 9

Finn

I STAYED.

Right there in that vast house with Cameron. We were doing something so normal. We'd settled on a made-for-TV movie, with a shitty script and even worse acting.

I was nervous, but the movie stopped me at least thinking about worst-case scenarios, as I relaxed enough to lose myself in the world of make believe.

I nudged Cameron. "Watch—her ex will come in just when she's saying the wrong thing." He chuckled. Encouraged that he wasn't pissed I'd interrupted the film and feeling all the warm and fuzzies as a consequence, I carried on with my thoughts. The actress was doing an entire speech containing her entire life story, including the very secrets she wanted to keep from her ex, when said ex walked in the room and cleared his throat. "Called it!" I snapped my fingers. "And now there will be the big misunderstanding." I glanced at Cameron, who was staring at me and not the screen. I felt weird. "Shit, did I spoil that for you? I do this kind of thing all the time, y'know second-guessing the scripts and scrutinizing for cheese levels, you can stop me if you don't want me to—oomph—"

He kissed me, and of course, that one touch turned to another, and there was addictive freedom in losing myself in the taste of a man. No one could see us, no one was judging me, and it was all because this gorgeous, sexy, man.

By the time we broke apart, he was sprawled in my lap, my hands on his ass, his arms around my neck, and at first, it was to share kisses, and then laughter, followed by hot, buttery popcorn as we separated to watch the movie. Our lip action didn't move on to more, but that was fine, because somehow we were both content to be near each other.

It felt right.

Real.

But wrong if I took too much time to think about it.

Like, what was I doing here?

Was this only sex, or is this sex with added movies, or was this a hookup, or friends with benefits?

Are we friends?

We've only known each other a few days.

Am I rushing into something that I'm going to regret?

Atlas will kill me—we still don't have an NDA that covers this.

I wish my brain would stop.

We ended up separating long enough for him to clamber off me, all lazy and happy, then for us to lean against each other, content to be touching. Until he slid down enough for me to put my arm over his shoulder. and I cuddled him, properly pulling him into my side and holding him close. Then, because I was nervous and a freaking mess, I went into what I like to call default Finn mode, which is rambling on about everything and nothing. I detailed my thoughts on the entire movie, and sometimes Cameron asked me questions about filming, and I did even more talking. He never once shushed me, or laughed at me, but as time went on, my squirrel brain was darting about, going from relaxed to stressed, from enjoying the moment to worrying. Should I ignore the nagging thought that he was being nice to me because he wanted something from me? It wasn't money. I understood he had more than enough of that, and his home was magnificent, but maybe an agent introduction. Or was it only sex?

I mean, it *was* fantastic sex.

I managed a handful more popcorn because it was so ingrained in me to stay away from anything that might wreck the abs, although I did spend a short time reasoning that sex burned off more calories than I'd be consuming. Then, for some crazy reason, my brain decided to contemplate my exit strategy. I don't know why my instincts told me I needed to leave—maybe it was my *actual* brain taking over from the one in my pants after a self-preservation switch was thrown. I should listen to my instincts, after all, if Atlas found out I'd done this with Cameron without an NDA, he'd go ballistic. All I knew was that as soon as the credits began to roll on a ludicrous ending, I was itching to leave.

"I should go." I scooted back, picking at popcorn in my lap.

"You don't have to."

"I probably do. Sorry."

"That's okay," Cameron said, then tilted my chin, so I was meeting his gaze instead of staring at the remainder of my snack sticking to my T-shirt. "You don't need to apologize for needing to leave. I'll see you tomorrow at the rink, and then after, maybe we could—"

"I think we should stop doing that."

He made a face like a goldfish, and wariness filtered into his expression. "Because of what happened between us?" he asked in a regretful tone.

"You're too much of a temptation," I whispered.

"Back at you." He smiled at me. "Maybe I can find someone else to help you, someone on the team who won't want to kiss you."

"I don't want anyone else," I said without thinking.

"So, we're good to keep going."

If we were doing the hockey, then I wouldn't have to be doing the talking, and maybe I could re-learn how to skate, and everything would be okay.

"Yeah," I said, then slumped back and, this time, I stared at the TV, which had gone into sleep mode. All I could see was a reflection of me being the awkward idiot I am and gorgeous sexy Cameron being... well, being gorgeous and sexy. We were so different, and I don't mean only in looks, with my blond thing against his hot—burning hot—dark-eyed devil. I was deep in the closet, and he was free of all that. I mean, he marched in LA Pride for fuck's sake, and I knew that because there were photos of him and some of the other team members all waving flags on the Storm's social media. I'd never even seen a Pride parade up close, let alone joined in with the love.

"Did I say something wrong?" he asked.

The need to leave poked at me from nowhere, and my chest got all tight. This was the moment he asked me if I was okay, and then, I'd have to make exaggerated excuses about why I was quiet. "No."

"It's just that you've gone strangely quiet," he murmured.

"Sorry."

"It's all good. I like just sitting with you."

Okay. He doesn't want me talking. Message received. Not that I had anything else to say right now. I was in my liminal space, that time when I knew I needed to move on to the next thing; in this case, I should be leaving.

"Sorry for talking too much." And then going quiet.

"About movies? I loved that. Don't get me started on hockey. Next time, we'll watch a game, and I'll explain everything."

Next time? Was there going to be a next time?

What about when he realized his comment on me being quiet was hitting the nail on the head. I could handle interactions, hell I could handle an entire movie, but the downtimes when I was chilled, that was the other side of me—the person I became after I'd run out of vibrant excitable *me*. It happened all the time, people meeting me, chancing upon me on a day when my social well was full, and then finding out that any kind of social brilliance they thought I had was a pretense.

It was happening now. All the positive stuff about movies, and me joking with him, was being replaced by worries filling the empty space where relaxed and happy should be. Freaking social anxiety crippled me, and it came from nowhere. I wanted to sit and hug, but Cameron was *normal*, and he said I was quiet, and that was something I needed to address. Right?

Maybe we should just have sex again because we don't have to talk when we're fucking... making love... whatever.

People who met me when I could channel the star of an action franchise—confident, strong, saves the world. But once the hellos were over, all I had was the uncanny ability to talk their ears off about movies, and then luckily, I could move on to the next person.

But one-on-one interactions? They were hard.

And I'd already shown Cameron my particular skill of dissecting a script. So now what? Give him some impromptu acting lessons to fill the quiet space?

"I'm not sure I can do this," I said, but not to him, more to myself.

"Watch movies?" he joked.

I wish he would stop joking and listen to me.

How can he be serious when you're not explaining anything?

He nudged me, and I glanced up and fell into the warm beauty that was his dark eyes. His socket was bruised, the center of the wound darkening, but it didn't take away from how sexy he was. "We had fun," he said. "I'd like to have *fun* again, but I get the feeling maybe you're done with this now. And that's cool as well. You do you." I wasn't sure he meant that last part, given he cradled my face and stared right into my eyes.

"You don't know the real me, and doing this again means that you'll see everything." Fuck. Where had that come from? Had I warned him off? Or exposed my soft belly ready to be ripped apart?

"Well, the *real* you has weak ankles," he murmured and kissed me again, and somehow the urge to run quietened inside me.

"And ADHD," I admitted in a whisper.

His eyes widened momentarily, but then he nodded. "Okay."

Wait. Was that all he was going to say? Where were the questions or comments?

"Okay, and?"

"Thank you for telling me," he said and smoothed his thumbs over my cheekbones. "Our coach's daughter, Meghan, has ADHD, and sometimes she just needs to be alone and doesn't want anyone messing with her. I learned that the hard way, good old Uncle Cameron teasing her and pushing things too far at a cookout a few years ago. I grew up teasing other kids; that was how my siblings and I related. Anyway, Coach sat me in a chair and explained impulse control, and masking, and the overwhelming desire of Meghan wanting to be on her own, and all the spaces in between." He added another smile. "I'm a much better friend, now."

I waited a beat. "So, if I said I needed space, you wouldn't need to dissect why."

"Sure."

"Because it doesn't mean I don't want to be here. I do, but maybe I shouldn't be here because it's a step too far, and it feels like I'm jeopardizing my movie roles, but then, movies aren't real and..."

Cameron pressed one final kiss to my nose. "I'll see you at the rink in the morning."

"You still want to do that?"

"Tomorrow. Nine a.m. I'll bring coffee; you bring breakfast."

He walked me to the door, giving me a lingering kiss, before standing back as I walked to my car. Impulsively, I stopped and went back to him.

"I have other movies I can show you."

He grinned and held out a fist, which I bumped. "I'd like that."

"Tomorrow, then."

"Tomorrow."

I pulled out onto the main road with caution, waiting until I was sure no go-karts were careening down the hill, and then, I headed home. We didn't live that far apart, no more than a few miles as the crow flies, but to get to my place, I needed to go toward the freeway before heading back up into my area of the hills.

I'd told him who I was. I'd had sex with him. I showed him my rambling self, and then my quiet side, and he didn't judge me, *and* he still wanted to see me tomorrow.

I call that a win, and even if we never had sex again, maybe I'd found a friend.

I sure hoped we had sex again.

Chapter 10

Cameron

I woke up a week later, my head fuzzy, and not from a night out at some exclusive club or from staying up too late with a new hook-up. I'd not even thought about anyone other than Finn since... well... since that day he'd followed me from the barn. Talk about something even scarier than testicular torsion. Being so zoned in on one lover was terrifying. And annoying, as I'd been pretty good at avoiding entanglements of any romantic nature for all of my adult life.

Now, here I was, lying in bed, my head filled with cotton batting as I battled to figure out how to balance being with Finn more, while keeping an emotional distance from him. I'd grown addicted to his presence in my life in a short amount of time. Our nights filled with Netflix and calling for Korean takeout home delivery—we both had a mad passion for sesame beef— had flipped some sort of domesticity button in my brain. Something my brother had told me would happen one day. Which sucked because now I'd have to admit that Lyle was right about something. Hopefully, not to his face though. Just to myself, which was possibly as bad.

So now, it seemed like I woke up, and the first thing I thought about was Finn. Like right now. My head was filling with dreamy little snippets from last night's movie. Some old Ryan Reynolds flick where he worked in a restaurant, which had some killer funny bits, and Ryan himself, which was enough to hold my attention on most occasions. Seems not even Mr. Reynolds could keep my gaze, hands, or mouth, off Finn Kerrigan. After mutual blow jobs, you would think I'd be filled up on Finn. Nope. Point in case--me lying here thinking of Finn.

Also, someone was hammering on the sliding door of my bedroom in a steady two-handed beat that made me want to open the glass door and boot the asshole off the patio.

"Hey, I can see you in there lying in bed!" Rottie called as he pounded out the drumbeat from what I assumed was one of his loud as fuck metal songs. Probably from a new album or video. Rottie appearing on my patio was nothing new. Fences meant nothing to him. He was a brazen-as-hell wild man who thought nothing of scaling canyon walls as well as security fences, and *seemed to think everyone needed a Rottie Blade in their house.* "Come on, Chavkin, roll out. I have a neighborly issue to discuss with you!"

I moved to my side, squinting at the tall, lanky rocker with long white and black hair pulled into a top knot. That was a new look. He stood on my patio in a green kilt that hung off his lean hips, his tattooed chest bared, wearing yellow hiking boots and a grin. The bastard was stupid hot. And stupid annoying.

I held up a middle finger, then, in slow increments, I kicked the covers aside and plodded to the patio. I did have things to do today, thank Christ, like spend time with my charity. Call home. Start reading over a script for a local food delivery service endorsement ad that I had to shoot. Which sucked because I was not an actor in the least, and my last commercial had been the subject of memes --where my face had been replaced by a famous wooden puppet-- for months.

I stared through the glass at Rottie, taking note of the grappling hook snugged tight on the railing. I pointed to it, and he shrugged innocently, a sweet-as-corn-syrup smile on his handsome face.

With a sigh, I unlocked the door and slid it open. A rush of warm dry air hit me.

"What the actual hell, Blade?" I snapped as he stepped into the air-conditioned coolness of my bedroom, then threw himself to my bed, his kilt flying up to show me and the world what he had been born with, and it was pretty substantial, not going to lie. "No, please, come on in and make yourself at home.

Would you like me to fetch you a cool drink? You must be parched having scaled not only the canyon, but my fence."

He chortled, folded his inked hands on his sweaty chest, and rolled those famed green eyes to me. Those eyes had been on the cover of his last chart-topping album, *Smiling Skulls of Mandalay* by his band, Pink Mail Schism, and people around the world had rushed out to apply eyeliner just like Rottie Blade did.

"I detect a note of sarcasm in your offer, Cameron."

I closed the door with some attitude, then stalked over to my dresser to find some underwear. There was no need to be shy around Rottie. We'd hooked up once when he'd first got the place next door. Which was why I'd not blinked at the sight of his junk. The man was a tornado in bed, but not at all my kind of lover after the deed was done. Not that I knew what my kind of lover after the deed was done was. Lover meant something long-term, right?

"Nice cakes," he called as I hoisted a pair of blue briefs over my ass.

"Thanks. Skating works wonders." I turned to face him. "What are you doing here?"

"I wanted to let you know that my camel, Scheherazade, got loose and was last seen heading your direction, so I thought I'd come see if you'd seen her."

"You lost your camel?"

"Yep." He sat up, his kilt sliding down to cover his balls, and stared out of the window with utter dejection. "I had some friends over last night for a go-kart race -- sorry I didn't invite you, but you still don't have a kart -- and some chick that my drummer is banging…" He chuckled at his own joke.

"Right, drummer, banging. I get it. Go on." I needed him to speed things up so I could shower and wash Finn out of my thoughts.

"Right, so this chick got a little hyper from all the Skittles and wandered into the camel and zebra enclosure." Of course. The zebras. I'd heard their brays a few times when the wind was blowing correctly. But I'd never heard a camel. Did camels make noise? "She got scared when Sherry -- that's what I call Scheherazade for short -- got upset by a stranger stumbling up to her, and spit in her hair. The girl freaked out and ran out of the pen leaving the gate open. We rounded up the zebras and Barry the bison, but Sherry is still at large. Have you seen her?"

"Your camel?"

"Yes, my camel. Are you slow-minded since that crushing loss to Boston?"

"No, fuck off. I have other shit on my mind; and no, I have not seen or heard your camel." I made a motion to the patio door. A short, but curt wave of my hand indicating he could leave now.

"Oh, okay, it's romance-related right? You got the look." I blinked at the rock star who was now tapping out and humming "U Got the Look" on his bare thighs. "Prince was a god."

"Yeah, he was," I concurred because he had been.

"So, what's his or her name?"

"Nope, no, not discussing my sex life with you." I waved at the door again. With more gusto, Rottie sighed with added drama, then sprang to his yellow hiking boots. "I'll keep an eye out for your camel. Now if you would, please take your mountain-climbing gear and go back home."

"Fine, but if you keep all that emotional baggage locked up inside, your skull will explode from the sheer power of love and guts." His green eyes flared. "Damn that's a good line. If you see Sherry, just offer her some apple wafer cookies, and lead her home, will you? Thanks, you're a peachy man."

He kissed me on the mouth, then left, tossing a leg over the railing, exposing his junk once more, before disappearing down the rope. I waited, then stepped out, glanced down, and saw him staring up at me.

"Toss down my hook!" he bellowed.

I did. He jumped out of the way, saluted me, then dove into a dune buggy the color of a flamingo and raced off, kicking up dust and stones in his wake.

"Note to self. Add barbed wire to the top of the security fence."

I rushed through a fast breakfast and workout, then hustled my way to my garage, choosing to take my Jeep, instead of the Mercedes. I wanted to feel the wind in my hair. Maybe that would blow Finn Kerrigan out of my head. God knows the workout, shower, and food hadn't shifted his tasty ass from my thoughts.

Clocking that I was already running late, I sighed in exasperation when I got to the end of my driveway and there stood a camel eating the rhododendron that grew beside the gate. Scheherazade stared at me with disdain after I called to her to move. She refused. I cussed my neighbor out as I dialed Rottie. Then, I cussed him out over the phone.

He arrived twenty minutes later on the back of a zebra with some dude with tattoos on his face—a skinny white dude with a large green afro wearing a beaded skirt and rainbow Crocs—and led his camel home after gifting me with a pink snapback cap with the band name on the front.

Moving to a new Rottie-less neighborhood was looking better and better, although the pink cap was pretty tight. I wore it to the rink where it got all kinds of comments from the kids, and the adults as well. Prez and Charlie were here, which was always a big thrill. Any time one of the Storm showed up, let alone two—aside from me because I was old hat to the kids—they were super excited.

We had about forty kids in the club now. I'd been sponsoring it for about three years, and at first, it had been tough to lure the kids in—hockey is still considered to be a white man's sport, so lots of POC kids were hesitant—but after seeing how much fun skating was, our numbers began to grow. Of course, we had other sponsors now, including the Storm, a national health insurance company, Cali Natural Gas, and local credit unions, as well as several youth hockey organizations. I still bought all the gear for the kids and did my best to be here as often as possible.

"Nice hat," Prez called as we herded kids into their age groups while parents settled in the stands for the first practice of the summer session. "I didn't think you were into metal. I thought you were a big Manilow-head."

Charlie sniggered, and I threw him a death stare. You get caught humming "Copacabana" one time and never live it down.

"Go rock on a pony," I said, the comeback not at all the one I wanted to use. I flipped him off mentally. "Rottie is my neighbor, and I helped him find his camel so—"

"'Camel'?" Prez asked while volunteers tried to harness the energy in the rink. We had a long-term contract with this older, but still solidly built ice palace. Back in the day Hollywood starlets would come here to skate. There were pictures on the walls of famous starlets and leading men all glamorous as they cut figure eights into the ice.

"Yeah, long story."

Prez got dragged away. and then, it was just me and Charlie waiting to start. He seemed distracted, and I was right that something was on his mind when he leaned in and spoke to me in a quiet voice.

"Can I ask you something?"

"Sure."

"Little Mikey is off grid; you haven't heard from him have you?"

"You lost your brother?"

"Not lost him. I mean, I see the lights on in his place, but he's not being social and shit."

"That's probably because you call him Little Mikey. Why can't you call him Zeetoo like the rest of us?"

Charlie winced and muttered something under his breath that I had no way of hearing in the chaos. Then, he shrugged. "I'm sure it's all good." He didn't sound convinced, but he grabbed his stick. "Let's do this thing."

I smiled at one of the volunteers, Miles, a tall guy with lots of gold curls. He gave me a glance that simmered, but I merely nodded at one of the kids right beside him with an untied lace. Sure. Miles was cute, but his eyes weren't blue enough, and his face was too long. Also, and I know this is a total Seinfeld schtick, but the guy was a sentence-finisher. Finn always let me complete my sentences. When I turned back to speak to Prez, he didn't hide that he was assessing me. "What? Did I miss a patch of whiskers when I shaved?"

I patted at my cheeks. I *had* been rushed thanks to mountaineer Blade showing up at the ass crack of my day.

"No, you just got this dorky look on your face like

you saw a unicorn or found free Manilow tickets on the ice."

"Don't you have kids that need your expertise on something over by the net?" I asked as I waved a gloved hand at one end of the ice.

"What's her or his name?" Prez pushed, his stick resting on his thick neck as his hands draped over opposite ends.

"Why is everyone asking me that today?!" My teammate shrugged. "There is no he or she, I don't do that kind of sh... shiny newts." Two little girls with pigtails wobbled past, cheeks plumped from their ear to ear grins. "So, Viking chic?"

Prez chuckled. "Coward, changing the subject. We'll find out eventually." No, they—and by "they" I meant the team—would not because Finn was firmly closeted, and I was firmly averse to commitment. "I have no idea what that even means. You know Charlie and his theme parties. For his birthday, it was *Great Gatsby*. The time before that, he threw that adult prom party. Oh, and then there was the camping party where he wore a sleeping bag all night. But this one is all his brother's fault, apparently."

"I have no clue what a chic Viking wears. Skinny jeans to match his horned helmet?" I was clueless. Charlie was a great guy, a fantastic player, and one of our Storm rainbow brethren, but his party ideas were ridiculous, and with Zeetoo getting in on them as well, this was shit.

"Yeah, maybe. Hey, I bet the person you got dopey-looking over might have an idea. Are you bringing them?"

Honest to Gretzky, the guy was like a dog with a fucking femur. I shook my head, then, thank goodness, was saved from further interrogation by twenty or so kids of about ten gathering around me. I gave Prez a smug little smirk, then led my ducklings—all in bright purple sweaters with their CC's Club team logos on the front—to a corner of the rink. Many of them were veterans of the organization, but a few were new faces. They were bright and attentive, eager to learn the basics of the game that, until this inner-city league, they'd been unable to afford. Hockey was not a cheap game to play, especially for kids who outgrew equipment every year or two. My parents could attest to that. Also, traveling from game to game was hard on working parents, which was why we also provided transportation to away games. I'd been happy to sign the check for a few vans. The dealer we'd bought them from offered me a contract to do commercials on the spot, which I was pleased to sign after my agent read it over. I then bought my Mercedes from him, made four spots, and got trolled for my acting ability.

As I put the kids through some simple drills, my thoughts kept slipping back to a certain actor and a certain party. Would Finn want to go if I asked him? Charlie *had* said to bring a date...

Not that Finn would be there as my date, obviously,

but as a buddy. We could pull that off with ease. A couple of friends—no benefits—just hanging out with a bunch of jocks. How heteronormative could you get? No one would think a thing about him being there. If we told the guys that I was helping him with a role in a hockey movie that would cement the lie.

Someone fell down beside me, began crying, and that jarred me from my daydreams about me and Finn going out in the world together. I hoisted the little girl up to my hip. She reminded me of my little sister. She clung to me until her mom showed up to take her.

"You're so good with the kids. When are you going to have some of your own?" Mom of the Crying Child asked.

I mumbled some words about skate blades. She nodded, then carefully moved across the ice with her daughter in her arms. The little girl gave me a timid wave that I returned.

Kids? Me? Pfft. Yeah, no, not anytime soon. Kids required time, love, and commitment. I seemed to be lacking in most of those key areas I'd been told more than a few times by more than a few people. Mostly, people I'd left after getting my itch scratched. Love and commitment required time, and as we had covered just a moment ago, I had little of that so…

Nope to kids right now. Maybe later. After hockey. When I had a partner.

My life was fine at the moment. Me and Finn were doing good… if you called hiding and lying good.

Which I did, right? Sure. I was happy with things. No strings. Lots of sex. A few cuddles. Tons of takeout food. Yep, it was the perfect arrangement.

So why the hell was I already tapping out a text to Finn? Had my fingers been possessed? I hit send before I could change my mind. Great, now I was rebelling against my better judgment. What kind of spell had Finn Kerrigan cast on me? A finger enchantment maybe? I stared at the sent text. Shit, he had already seen it. Too late to delete it now. *Fuck*. Now came the dread of waiting for a reply. Maybe Rottie was right. Maybe the loss to Boston had given me slow mindfulness…

HEY. WANT TO GO TO A PARTY ON FRIDAY NIGHT? *NOT A DATE! Just as buddies. ~ CC*

Chapter 11

Finn

"YOU CAN DO THIS." I TOLD MY REFLECTION. I'D TAKEN my meds, found my center, drank herbal tea, worked through all the worst-case scenarios, and then dressed as my nerd-fantasy, Thor.

It was movie-Thor, or at least my version of Chris Hemsworth's Thor, who was staring back at me now, complete with fake hammer, long blond wig that Jimmy-K had weaved into my own hair, and make-up that accentuated my cheekbones.

Or that was what Jimmy-K said the makeup did, and as he reminded me that he *was* an artist to the stars. He'd made me look good in all three *Rapid* films, so I had to trust him. He'd just left, after assuring me that naked chest was a good look on me, and that I'd be pushing people away with a stick.

Or a hammer.

The man had jokes.

I swear there should have been more to this outfit— Chris Hemsworth had a black bodysuit under the swirling cape, whereas all I had were snug dark pants along with bare chest? I guess I should have been thankful that at least the groin was covered with this leather flap thing, because otherwise people would be able to tell which way I dressed.

"I'm sure Hemsworth wasn't naked from the waist up," I pointed out to my reflection, and readjusted the cloak over the bondage-like leather harness that was all I had to cover any of my front and sides. Thankfully, the cloak was big, and I could pull it around myself, but I was second-guessing going to this party dressed like this. Only, Cameron had said Viking chic, and this was my best interpretation, and with me being similar in size and build to the Thor actor, it should work out okay.

"People will look at you and see a poor second to Chris freaking Hemsworth," I muttered. "Maybe I shouldn't go as Thor." Hell, I was second-guessing going at all.

"Fuck you!" I snapped at my indecisive self, wishing I could muster up some impulsive confidence to carry me through this. Instead, I was a bundle of nerves at meeting the entire Storm hockey team. Or at least whoever of the team was left in LA right now, and wondering if maybe—hopefully—this might be the start of something real with Cameron.

As real as it could ever be when I'm in the fucking closet.

"Suck it up, Kerrigan!" I warned, then practiced smiling and giving the hammer a few swings. Jimmy-K had smeared some kind of shimmery oil on me, and god, way to look like an idiot.

The buzzer sounded for the gate, and I headed to one of the house screens and buzzed in Cameron, who was coming to pick me up. He was driving a convertible; the camera angle was bad, but he pulled on fake Viking horns as he clambered out and walked up the steps to the door. I should have gone downstairs and let him in, but instead I wavered. He was dressed in simple black, no cloak, no bare chest, whereas I'd called in makeup and wardrobe.

Fuck my life. *Why am I so extra?*

Maybe if I didn't go down, he'd leave after a while, and I wouldn't have my Thor-persona seen by anyone at all.

He knocked, and I knew he expected me to be there, but as usual, my brain decided to ramble and mess things up, and instead of being down there like a sensible *buddy*, I was up here staring at a mirror. I grabbed my phone and sent him a quick message.

Have to cancel. Sorry.

He didn't reply, but he didn't knock again, and his car was still there. What was he doing? Sitting on the porch waiting for me? I rolled my eyes at half naked me and placed the hammer with great care on my vanity.

I heard footsteps, a door opening and closing, and knew he'd let himself in.

I really should go downstairs.

"Holy fucking Gretzky, and hell, no!" Cameron exclaimed from my bathroom door, causing me to lose at least three lives as I spun to face him, my scarlet cloak billowing around me and my hand on my chest right over my heart.

I smoothed the cloak. "Cameron!"

"No way am I letting you go to the party looking like that!" He turned to leave the bathroom, and I didn't follow him, my heart sinking. I'd seen that look before, when I'd fucked up with something that seemed fine at the time of doing it. Awkward Finn is awkward.

"I'm sorry!" I called after him.

Fuck, I'd had so many years with people dressing me for parts I'd never even thought that—

"You need to put this on! Stat." Cameron returned, and I got a real eyeful of the sexiest Viking I'd ever seen. Of course, I hadn't seen many Vikings at all, apart from on the silver screen, but Cameron -- in his tight black shirt and hip-hugging pants, with his stubble and god, was that eyeliner? -- was a walking advertisement for sex. He held out a black T-shirt, but as I reached for it, he cursed under his breath, dropped it to the floor, and tugged me into his arms, then kissed me, pushing me back into the vanity and pinning me as he went to his knees. "I've never seen anything like you..." He unzipped my pants and eased them over my hips.

"I didn't fuck up?" I asked him as he yanked at the leather as it stuck to my skin, and inhaled sharply when he tugged aside my thong—the only thing keeping my cock in place.

"Beautiful," he whispered, and cradled my balls as he licked from the base to the tip of my cock. He kept talking, and praising, and telling me that I was too much for others, and that he wanted me himself, and then, I couldn't hear him at all as I was moaning and writhing, and when he swallowed me whole, I shoved away the horns and gripped his short dark hair, holding him still so I could get my head straight, then releasing a little as he slid his fingers to my ass, one tapping my hole, his lips and tongue hot.

"Close," I warned.

He groaned around my cock, and it was game over as he swallowed everything I gave him. I scrabbled to hold on, lost in my orgasm, aware he was still holding me in place, one hand on my chest, the other pulling his cock out, getting himself off as he kissed me.

"Fuck," he leaned on me where I could feel his hand stripping his cock, and then he was arching and coming, then stumbling away, his back hitting the far wall.

He waited, breathing heavy. I tossed him a towel, which he caught in midair with his mad reflexes. He tucked himself away, but I didn't move to do the same —it had taken oil to get me in these pants and I wasn't sure I'd get them up again.

"Hi?" I was saying hello, but it was also a question, and he raised an eyebrow, his breathing ragged.

"Hi?" he repeated. "You're in here wearing bondage gear and literally nothing else, and that's all you have to say."

"It's not bondage." I peered at the harness. "At least I don't think it is." I swirled my cloak a little, the material brushing my naked ass. "I have this."

He stalked over to me, kissing me as he unbuckled the harness holding the voluminous mass of scarlet material and let it slip to the floor. Then, he picked up the T-shirt, taking his time pulling it over my head, careful not to touch the hair, then lifting the mass of twisted blond wig out of the way and smoothing the dark cotton over my chest. He examined the harness, buckled it, clipped the cloak, and stepped back. I wiped cold cum from my skin then inched up the leather pants until they were at least over my hips. I was way too sensitive to tuck my cock back in, and I sent him a rueful smile.

"We probably need to wait."

"You're so beautiful," he muttered. He stepped into my space, helping me close the fastener on the pants, smoothing my cloak. "I don't want to share with the rest of my team." He rested his forehead on mine. "Some of the team would have eaten you alive, not to mention anyone else that got to see all that skin, you should have a warning tattooed on you."

"Um, thank you?"

"Shit." He stepped back again, and even though I tried to reach for him, he avoided me as if he were on the ice, smooth and fast and untouchable. "I just went all beast mode on you."

"Yep."

"I did that." He waved at me, then at the hammer, which was now on the floor split in two. "And that."

"It was great."

"I don't get territorial like that," he half-whispered. "I'm sorry."

Now it was my turn, and I crowded him against the wall, cupping his groin and pressing there. "Mine," I muttered against his lips. "All mine."

He groaned, I sagged, and we were kissing again, but this time it was lazy, changing the tempo, learning the things we liked, taking our time. His cell vibrating pulled us from the stupor of post-orgasm loving, and he pulled it out with a rueful smile as he read the message.

"We're late," he said, and kissed me again, slowing the licks and sucks until we just hugged. He was small in my arms, and he wasn't a small man at all, he was strength and corded muscles, and he was all mine.

For the moment.

"So much for indestructible metal, forged in the heart of a dying star," he muttered as he picked up the broken hammer where Styrofoam blocks from the interior had fallen out.

"Wait, what?"

He tried to slot the two main pieces together, then gave up and dropped them into the trash can.

"I might have this thing for super heroes," he admitted with a grin. "And now, when I think of Thor, all I'll see is you oily and shiny, half naked and wearing leather."

That deserved another kiss, and I had words I wanted to say on the tip of my tongue.

That I liked superheroes.

And that when he'd sucked me off, it was clear he had a super-tongue.

But how awkward would that make me?

Way too awkward.

THE HOUSE WE PULLED UP AT WAS AN EXPANSE OF WHITE, with a landscaped turning circle and probably a million gorgeous cars lined up. Cameron's low-slung Porsche wasn't out of place as he parked it next to a stunning scarlet Ferrari, which I stopped to admire after we climbed out.

"Nice." I let out a low whistle and bent as much as I could in these unforgiving pants to check out the dash and the acres of butter-soft cream leather. "SF90 Spider," I added and ran a hand gently over the paintwork.

"That's Prez's new baby."

"Prez?"

"Brett Kennedy aka Prez; he's a buddy, and all we heard two months back was the sad sorry story of how a bird pooped on the seat. If he corners you, ask him about it. Also, I'm warning you now, Charlie loves his movies, and I know he's watched the *Rapid* movies, so I'm sorry in advance if he asks too many questions—"

"I can handle questions," I interrupted.

He reached for me on instinct, then dropped his hand. "Buddies," he muttered to remind himself. "No touching." He leaned toward me, but not so close it would seem odd to anyone who cared to notice. "But I can still taste you on my tongue."

"You can't say things like that," I whined. "My cock likes it too much, and these pants don't stretch."

He chuckled, then squared his shoulders as if he was going into battle. "So, yeah, this is Charlie's place. He's like the captain of the cheer team, always optimistic and talking the guys up. Good guy who loves hosting the big meet-ups, families, kids, the whole team. His brother is Zeetoo, adopted brothers before you ask, so they don't look alike—he's a big Harlequins fan."

I stared at him blankly. "Harlequins?"

"Y'know, the LA Harlequins. Football. Funny-shaped balls."

"Oh, yeah," I felt foolish because even I had heard of the city's much lauded football team.

"Oh, and Phillipe is our goalie, and he's just this insane mess of nonsense at times, and comes off as grumpy, but he's a teddy bear really and loves talking books."

I parsed all the data. "Okay so Prez is cars. Zeetoo is a football fan, specifically Harlots."

"Harlequins."

"Sorry, Harlequins. Charlie movies. Phillipe is a grumpy teddy bear and likes books. Anyone would think you're offering me conversation tips." I was joking, but he regarded me with soft affection.

"I want you to enjoy this, and I thought some of that might help. I want you to meet my friends." He smiled. "But not in a super creepy this-is-the-guy-I'm-messing-around-with kind of way, just in a..." He shrugged. "You know what I mean. *Buddy.*"

I wasn't sure I did. Part of me wanted more than the messing about part and to walk in as something more important to Cameron.

Like a partner, boyfriend, kind of thing.

Go figure.

Chapter 12

Cameron

This was an *incredibly* bad idea.

Also, I now know how it feels when I talk up other people's dates, and yeah, I'm not a fan. Not that the guys were flirting with Finn, and who was I to say jack squat if they were, because me and Finn were friends with some hidden hot AF bennies, but the guys were buzzing around him like flies. As were the ladies. And the kids.

Finn was giving Thor-type speeches and, to be fair, doing a damn good impersonation of Chris Hemsworth. The kids were enthralled. Many were caught up in the role-playing and were pretending to be Captain America, Iron Man, and Black Widow. One rebel was quoting *Deadpool*, which got him a timeout from his mother and a glare for his dad from his wife for letting the little guy watch *Deadpool* in the first place. Poor Alexie. He'd be flying back to Belarus with an irate spouse tomorrow. Unpleasant, to say the least. Which was why I didn't do wives, or husbands, or significant others. Why deal with all that side crap when all a man wanted was to get laid, have a snack, and take a nap. Oh, and play hockey and—

The fuck? Was Zeetoo making eyes at Finn?

I leaned to the left to stare around someone blocking my view. It was widely known in and out of the locker room that Zeetoo was bisexual. He'd dated one of Ariana Grande's backup dancers for the first year he was in LA, which caused a stir for about ten minutes, then the haters moved onto something else. Zeetoo *was* checking out Thor's hammer, the lech. I should just go over there and loop an arm around Finn to show—

"So did you get a rotten pepper?"

I snapped out of the ugly green fog of jealousy to find Charlie—sporting a damn good character look from the *Vikings TV show*—staring at me curiously.

"What?" I asked, distracted by Zeetoo chuckling at something Finn had said. Granted, there were about twenty people surrounding Finn, including a pack of kids, but Zeetoo's attention on *my* man—and yes I wanted to call him mine—was a little *too* attentive.

"The dip." Charlie pointed to the glob of guacamole sitting on a chip about four inches from my mouth. How long had that been there? I stuffed the food in and chewed. "You were holding it and hovering, and I thought maybe you found a bad jalapeño."

"Nope," I said after swallowing. "Good dip."

"Thanks, I got the recipe from Zeig's wife, Rosa. She said her grandmother makes the best guac, and man was she right!"

"Totally the best dip," I replied, listing to the left to try to see around our back-up goalie, Ryan Sahin -- who was done up as Hiccup from *How to Train Your Dragon*, complete with a small Toothless stuffed dragon on his shoulder -- to find Finn but he had disappeared.

"I see you found Zeetoo." I snarked and nodded his way.

Charlie's smile dipped for a moment, but then he was nudging me and changing the subject.

"The kids love your date," Charlie said. The comment hit me hard. My eyes flared as my head whipped in Charlie's direction.

"He is not my date. Finn is not my date. We're friends, that's all. Why would you say that?" I replied with as much calm as I could muster. Charlie gave me a glance that screamed I was protesting too much. I chilled things down. "I mean, do I look like the kind of person Finn Kerrigan would date? Not that he'd date me because I'm a guy, and he's straight, and... yeah."

"Hey, I didn't mean anything. We're all queer here at the dip table," he replied as he waved a hand at Prez loading his paper plate with a pile of chips accompanied by at least a pound of guacamole. Phillipe was standing next to our team captain spooning some taco dip onto his plate while trying his best to keep his horned helmet on his head. Zeetoo, the flirt, was not here because he was… where had he gone now? "I just asked because your eyes have been glued to Finn since you arrived."

"No, they're not," I answered as I wiped my fingers on a napkin that read *VALHALLA BOUND*. Charlie went all-out for his parties.

"Yeah they are," Prez and Phillippe chimed in.

I shot them death ray stares that didn't even make them flinch. "No, they are not. Finn's just shy and not used to big parties," I lied.

Phillippe gawked at me. "A movie star who isn't used to big parties?" he asked, his pretty French-Canadian accent at total odds with his faux fur cape and plastic-horned battle helm outfit. "Is that not a cross up or… how do you say it? Mix-up? Crossed purpose?" He sighed then repeated himself in French, which cleared things up not one bit.

All three men at the dip table stared at me as if I had a longship resting atop my head.

"No, it is not. Not everyone who's an actor likes to be in big crowds," I replied with a little more vinegar than I should have. Prez, Charlie, and Phillippe all exchanged looks, then began mumbling about how I was right, they were wrong, and lots of stars disliked being with the public and the price of fame. Brad Pitt, Harrison Ford, hell the list was as long as my arm of famous people who talked freely about how being famous was not all it was cracked up to be. "He's straight. He's just a friend. I'm training him for a hockey role he wants to win, and he's helping me with my acting."

"Good thing. Those last commercials you did were painful," Prez said around a mouthful of spicy guacamole.

Charlie and Philippe nodded as they chewed.

"That is why we call you Pinocchio," Phillippe interjected as his horned helm slid over his eyes. The air filled with French curse words. "Stupid hat," he mumbled while shoving at his hat.

"Thank you for your kindness and supportive words," I tossed out.

Prez snickered as I stalked off to find Finn with no ulterior motive other than to check that he was okay among this sea of snarky jocks who needed to mind their own beeswax, as my father liked to say. Dad was big on bee jokes. He had a few hives in the backyard. God I missed him, and Mom, and my sister.

And I maybe sort of missed my older brother, Lyle. Just maybe sort of.

I stopped by the bar and ordered two Cokes with lots of ice from the caterer Charlie had hired. She smiled, winked, and handed me two glasses of soda along with a slip of paper with her number on it. I nodded at the pretty redhead, then headed outside and dropped the phone number into a potted plant on the way out of the door. I found Zeetoo, half hidden behind a yucca, on his phone, his expression tense, his brow furrowed. At least, if he was out here staring at his phone, then he wasn't messing with Finn.

"Sup?" I asked Zeetoo, who jumped a mile and hurriedly shut his phone, then gave me a shit-eating grin.

"Sup," he replied, then sauntered off in the opposite direction.

"Great talk," I muttered, then continued my search. I didn't have to search too long or too hard for my errant non-date-buddy. Finn was in the backyard, running in circles around several palm trees lit from the ground, as kids of various sizes chased him. Some, I assumed, were bad guys, or at least one was, as he had found a green tablecloth and a stick that he was brandishing like a weapon.

"I have glorious porpoises!" Little Loki yelled as he ran after Finn.

Resting my ass against the railing of a wide porch, I watched Finn and the children for several minutes, smiling at their hoots and hollers as they played out some version of a Viking tale I was not familiar with. Thor, Loki, and a tiny version of Black Panther were in charge of the world—which was a small-looking glass orb yard decoration—and had to ward off the other kids, aka bad guys from another planet. Finally, the world-saving ended when Loki was called inside by his mom because it was time to go home to bed. The other kids were rounded up as well, which left Finn standing in Charlie's tidy yard, panting and sweating, grinning like he had just won an Oscar.

I carried his soda over to him.

"Thanks," he huffed, taking the cold drink, then draining the red plastic cup in one long pull.

I watched his throat working as he drank, enjoying the movement of muscle as he swallowed. When his gaze met mine, his brilliant blue eyes sparkled with pleasure. My gut clenched as my breathing hiked. It was right then that I knew I needed some space. Friends didn't get this worked up over a smile. They didn't leap on their buddy in a bathroom in a fit of jealous insecurity. And they did *not* stalk their friend at a party for talking to another guy. This behavior was not me. I didn't know who it was, but Cam Chavkin it was not. And it terrified the living shit out of me.

"No worries."

"This has been really fun. Your teammates are so friendly and accepting of you being queer. It's... well, it's nice to see in a sport that is *so* macho."

"Yeah, they're great guys. The whole organization is working overtime to ensure that everyone can play the game. Inclusivity is important."

He nodded, then held up his empty plastic cup. We tapped them together as if they were champagne flutes and not red Solo cups.

"I will drink to that." He turned his attention to a small group of people who had meandered outside. We did the whole party schmoozing thing, making small talk, eating too much dip, and wishing Charlie had chosen a theme with less fur and horned hats because it was damned warm for pelts covering your body.

"... Stupid!" I heard someone yell and turned to see Charlie dragging his brother into the house, Zeetoo tugging back. Siblings. I feel the pain. I exchanged glances with Prez who shrugged in an "it's-Zeetoo-what-do-you-expect" kind of way.

Around midnight, I had to drag Finn away from his fans. He had signed a ton of autographs and taken hundreds of selfies.

"Oh hey, all the Storm players and their dates are tagging me on Insta," he commented as we drove home. The light from his phone illuminated his face as he smiled at the online interaction. I nearly ran up over the curb once as I was so fixated on him. He merely chuckled at the tire bump, then went back to his IG tags as I fumbled over some lame excuse about how my power steering fluid must be low. Feeling the heat in my cheeks, I forced myself to watch the road. I did not need to rear-end someone. Well, someone other than Finn. Which sounded good, to be honest. Maybe we both could use a good rear-ending. I knew I wouldn't mind it at all. My dick started to perk up as I drove, and by the time we were at his house, I was fully erect. Then, he turned to me.

"Thanks for a fun night."

"It was good to have you there."

"I like your friends. Your teammate Zeetoo told me this awesome joke about—"

I growled, coming over all territorial, which wasn't what we had going on at all, and his eyes widened. Then, he smiled and offered me his hand. And all the dirty thoughts vanished in a puff of cold gray smoke. Right, a handshake. Because we were still in buddy mode. I clasped his hand, shook it, and then, said something stupid.

"I'll escort you to your door."

Yep, that was the brilliance that is Cam Chavkin. As if this brute of a guy needed me to walk him to his stoop like he was a Georgia debutante.

"It's only forty feet," he pointed out. "But sure, if you want."

I did want. The night didn't feel as if it should be over yet. And so, in true gallant style, I rushed around the car, opened the door for him, and then, bowed at the waist.

Finn snorted at my nonsense, but allowed me to walk at his side to his front step. He turned to look at me after unlocking and opening the door.

"Did you want to come in?" I heard the subtle underlying question in that simple query. Yes, yes, hell yes, I wanted to come in. I wanted to lock the door on the outside world—the world that still scorned men loving other men—and free Finn from that burden. I wanted to hold him close, taste his skin, feel his body shudder as he found release... I wanted to lie beside him as he slept, then watch the sun cast his skin in deep golden rays.

That last bit put the fear of God into me. Cam Chavkin did not linger in bed with lovers. Knowing that Finn was different from all the others shoved an icy shiv into my heart.

"Yeah, I would, but I'm tired." I inserted a fake yawn. "I'll see you at hockey school tomorrow," I added to lighten the moment I had slaughtered.

"Oh, okay, that sounds good. I'm tired too. It's hard work being a god of thunder," he quipped, but I saw the disappointment in his eyes.

I smiled as best I could, then turned to head back to my car. I heard the door close, the knocker giving a barely there clatter as Finn pushed the door shut. I took another step, and then one more, then paused. Staring down at the smooth blacktop, I took a second to try to figure out what the fuck I was doing. What the hell was wrong with my brain to turn down an invitation so laced with carnal pleasures? I could leave before morning came. It would be simple. Fuck, then roll.

"You're an asshole, Chavkin," I growled, spun on my heel, and rushed to the heavy front door. I knocked once. The locks inside tumbled, and the door opened, as if Finn was just waiting on the other side for me to change my mind. Which I totally had. "Fuck that shit, I'm all yours." I nudged the door open wider, captured his face between my hands, and kissed the motherfucking daylights out of him. He melted into me, pulling me inside, mouths still sealed, and slamming the door on everything that was *out there*. In here, it was only me and Finn. That was more than enough. It was everything.

Chapter 13

Finn

CAMERON CAME BACK.

He was going to leave, and then he came back.

Did that mean something?

He'd left at the ass crack of dawn, but not before more tender kisses and a slap to my ass, and another kiss, and then some groping, and when his car lights vanished into the distance, I headed back inside and didn't know what to do with myself.

I stared at my script, the words swimming in front of me as I considered the party, his friends, the kids, and Cameron, him coming back. The single conclusion I could reach was that he was spooked, because he'd definitely started to run in the opposite direction, saying that he needed to sleep because he was tired. I could see through his words to the excuses beneath, and for a moment, my heart had cracked.

Stupid heart.

I thought dramatic cracks in the heart only happened in movie scripts and novels, but time stopped between the moment he'd waved me goodbye and when he knocked on the door.

That kiss had been everything.

More than everything—it had been a promise.

Or at least, that is what I was saying in return. I think.

And now, I was back to staring at the script and thinking that maybe I should clean the small fish tank in the kitchen even though I had a service for that. Or maybe I should wash my car? Nope, that had been done two days ago. I could put on some laundry. Clean the kitchen floors? I wandered from room to room, convinced I needed to do something that wasn't the thing I should be doing—reading the script. Procrastination, thy name is Finn Kerrigan, not to mention my thoughts were in full-on squirrel mode, so the doorbell startled me so bad I nearly fell on my ass turning to face the noise. Steadying myself, I headed down the hall—there was no one scheduled to be in the house, but I hoped that it was Cameron coming back again. Then kicked myself because he was long gone, and he doesn't know my gate code to let himself in.

I stopped then, and sent a quick text to him, debating over adding an x, when the doorbell sounded again.

"The fuck, Finn! I see you standing there!"

Shit. I'd gotten distracted, again.

Atlas sounded pissed, but that was my agent's default setting, so I wasn't too worried until I opened the door and saw his thunderous expression.

I let him in, and he grumbled and cursed as he toed off his shoes and stalked past me to the kitchen, then grabbed snacks out of my refrigerator. I watched bemused at his plate piled with everything from pickles and triangle cheese to a container of yogurt.

"I missed breakfast because of you," he explained with extreme prejudice, then made himself at home at my counter and spread his bounty before him. His dark eyebrows tangled as he dipped a pickle into the strawberry yogurt and munched down on that before gagging and checking out what he'd done. "Fuck my life and fucking protect me from fucking actors who eat fucking fucked-up pickles," he added, and shoved the jar away.

"Are actors who eat pickles a big problem? I mean, I don't actually eat pickles. I think they're leftover from a party," I started to ramble as I poured him a coffee, sliding it over to him, but keeping my distance. "I don't mind a gherkin here and there, and not in a sexual innuendo way, but anyway, morning—"

"Don't 'morning' me!" Atlas shuffled on the stool, close to slipping off one side, which led to another tirade of curses.

"Okay?" I prompted because it was obvious this was about me. "Did I do something?"

"It's more like what you aren't doing," he muttered,

and this time stuffed the triangle cheeses into the fruity yogurt which—yuck—but he seemed to enjoy it. The man was heading for an ulcer, and I took some of the guilt for that, because I'd done something else that had caused him to lose his shit.

I needed to clarify. What was he talking about?

"I didn't do, or not do, what? Or what? Or do? What?" Were we talking in circles?

He stopped with a cheese triangle halfway to his mouth, then used it to emphasize whatever point he was about to make. "Byrnes-Rose studios have offered you another ten million on top of their current offer, plus a bigger percentage share on turnover, *and* your input into the freaking storylines, just to get you to do *Rapid 4*, *and*, get this, they're throwing in a guaranteed *Rapid 5*, and I had to tell them no, so you owe me for not suggesting you do it." Everything fell out of him in run-on sentences, and it took me a while to parse that.

I blinked at my agent. 4 *and* 5? That was... I calculated it in my head; hell, that was a lot of money. Then it hit me that he'd said he *wasn't* here to convince me to do the movies; he *was* here to tell me he turned them down.

"So, you told them no?"

He sighed with such drama, then paced the kitchen, a bag of cherry tomatoes in his hand.

"They want to rapid release *Rapid Love* and *Rapid Danger*." He snorted at his own joke. "And I told them no, and when they asked if it was about more money, my agent heart began to wither and die." He pressed his free hand to his chest. "DIE! I tell you! Die!"

I shuffled to the side, getting the counter between me and him just in case he planned on using the bag of salad items as a deadly weapon.

"Okay, but why—"

"Why?" He pointed at me with his bag-carrying hand, a tomato escaping and flying across the kitchen to hit the coffee machine. I winced. "Because for some fucked-up reason, I like you, and agents shouldn't like their clients. Hell, I even feel affection for you." He rubbed his chest with his free hand as if that was the most awful thing on earth.

"I like you too," I murmured. "But—"

"You don't need four more years of hiding!" he shouted at me, and then the piss and vinegar disappeared from his voice. "Can a queer actor carry an action franchise? No. Not right now. If you sign on the dotted line, they'll screw you on the morality clause if you so much as step out of line. One innocent kiss caught on camera, and they'll label you as wrong. You come out as gay, or bi, or pan, or whatever you identify as—"

"Gay."

"That. You come out as gay, there is no way I can spin that to Byrnes-Rose and make it stick when you could cost them millions in box office receipts."

I tilted my chin and got all defensive. "I happen to think that being openly queer or not, I can carry two more movies." Wait. What was I saying? That was a lie —the movie world was a fickle and unforgiving mistress. Anyway, I didn't want to do any more *Rapid* movies. I wanted to make a name for my acting alone, *then* I wanted to come out.

I wanted to spend time with someone and not worry that my secret would spill.

Cameron. It's Cameron I want.

I deflated then, but the counter at my back held me up.

"Finn? Look at this." I glanced at Atlas, who was holding up a phone with a photo on it. He seemed to have calmed down, and I edged closer to check it out. The photo was an innocent one of me and Cameron at the party—me in my Thor outfit, kids in a circle around me, and Cameron laughing. I remembered that moment—it was a perfect second where I'd told a silly joke to the kids about Cameron and his inability to do cartwheels, and the children giggled and Cameron elbowed me, then proceeded to show me that yes, I was right, he couldn't do cartwheels.

The moment might have been innocent, but the photo was a different story. It was beautiful—Cameron grinning at me as I smiled back.

"It's a nice photo," I said, and I knew I sounded lame.

"It's all over social media."

"Okay, but—"

"Just be careful, because if I can see the way he's

looking at you, then others could. Head down, okay? Get through to full release on *The Cup*, and then after that, it's up to you to make the life you want. I'll make you the best most wanted gay actor in the entire world, but, please, for now, be careful."

"Okay."

THE WARNING ATLAS GAVE ME SPUN IN MY THOUGHTS AS I made my way to the rink to meet Cameron for today's lesson. I was getting better on a daily basis, working on the balance ball at home, and setting up a net in my basement. I'd even invested in some roller skates to scoot around my sprawling terraced gardens with their artful pathways. This huge area was about all I'd miss when I sold this place, and selling it was very much on the cards. My financial team was horrified when I suggested I sell, then said I should re-invest in property. I reminded them that I had invested in property, but it never became a home. Cameron's place was a home—this was just a house. A big empty house. The real estate agent was a friend of Atlas, who told me I'd get eight million for my place, and it would go in less than a day, and had pushed a load more details my way about bigger houses for me to move to.

I said I needed to think, and she huffed that the money would waste away in the bank.

But it wouldn't, if I started a charity like Cameron did with his hockey kids—how about an acting charity for kids? Or an acting hockey charity, or a hockey with actors charity or—

"Bend your knees, Finn!" Cameron barked in my ear, and I flailed, going from upright to ice in a second, sliding along the surface like a penguin and ending up in the net. Damn my brain and its momentary lack of attention to the real world.

"Goal!" I exclaimed as Cameron arrived at my side with an expression that mixed frustration and amusement.

"Where did you go?" he asked as he went to a knee next to me.

"Into the net, clearly." I said and sighed. "Did you know some goalies talk to their nets? I read about this one goalie, Russian, kind of sexy; he talks to his goalposts all the time. Sean Gunningdon-Loomin or something."

"Stan Gunnerson-Lyamin," I corrected. "You think he's sexy?"

"Well yeah, big, strong—"

He placed an icy glove over my mouth, and I spluttered.

"Have you stopped thinking about goalies I want to kill now?" Cameron asked.

I nodded. Then, I waved off his help and used the posts to stand, wiping at my face, the scent of glove way too intense. I wrinkled my nose, but the scent soon cleared when Cameron stole a kiss before skating away from me.

God, he's so sexy, with all that confidence, and his thighs, and hell—he's watching me back.

I struck a pose and fell on my ass again.

Fuck my life.

THREE WEEKS INTO LESSONS, AND CLOSER TO THE FIRST day of filming, I'd finally found my feet, or my skates, or whatever. I could start, stop, go backward, pivot, and the best bit of all, I could do that sexy sliding to a stop thing where ice is flicked up into the air. I made a mental note to suggest that as a close-up shot from the ground, but I bet River already had that in his head. It became so that, instead of skating and falling, I was skating and thinking about my character and how he would approach the ice.

And also, the script.

"Can I run some lines with you?" I asked, when, yet again, we ended up at his place, and he'd kissed me senseless as soon as I stepped in the door.

"Sure, I'd love to see it."

I tapped my lower lip. "I wonder if the NDA covers me sharing lines from the super-secret important script. Can I rely on your silence?"

He kissed me, pushing me back against the counter, and when my knees were so weak it was only him and the cupboards holding me up, he went for the kill with a full-on cradling-my-face-butterfly-kiss.

"I hope you know you can trust me."

And as I melted into his arms, I knew I could.

UNTIL THAT WAS, FIVE MINUTES INTO READING LINES, HE started laughing and wouldn't stop.

In fact, he was laughing so hard he snorted and rolled off the sofa, holding his belly.

"Pass me the puck—" he read, stopped, and then, the tears began.

Tears of laughter.

"What's funny?"

"No one politely says pass me the puck!" Cameron wheezed, and then snorted again, covering his face with his hands.

"What do they say then?" I checked the script, wondering if maybe I was not reading it right, but no, my character actually said, "pass me the puck." Maybe it was all about inflection.

"Please would you ever so kindly pass—" Cameron started with a fake British accent, and that made the laughing worse. He gasped, attempting to catch a breath, and made at least some attempt to chill, but it lasted only long enough until he pointed at the script and started all over again.

I straddled him on the floor, caught his hands, and stared down at him. "What *do* you say then?" I asked, smiling.

His laughing stopped, and he wriggled his hands free to reach up and cradle my face again.

"You're so beautiful," he murmured. "I want to kiss you all the time."

It was in that moment I fell in love.

I FOUND THAT LOVE WAS A TRICKY THING. AS ANOTHER week passed, and it was on the tip of my tongue to tell him, the read-throughs on the script became more important, and he worked with me on all the corny lines, which we smoothed out and sent back to the writers with the hope they would incorporate them.

Love was right there in my heart, but Cam was still my teacher, still a friend with benefits, still keeping my secrets. So, I focused on the movie and tried to ignore the uproar over rumors that the studio was looking for someone else to take on the *Rapid* franchise. My statement suggested I was moving to other projects, but a shit ton of people suggested that *Rapid*, plus the made-for-kids ladybug movie, were about the limit of my acting ability.

Whatever.

The contract for my part in *The Cup* was made public as well, and yep, there was a lot of gossip in which it was hotly debated about how shit I would be having a script that was more than one-liner quips. I knew I was better than that, my acting coach said he'd slap me upside the head if I even thought that I wouldn't be good in the part.

Cam said the same, between kisses and sex and a lot of laughter.

Knowing the role was mine made me work harder with Cam.

I'll show them.

And, according to him, hockey players tapped the ice to indicate that they were available, but most of the time, it was up to the passing player to go with instinct and know where other team members were.

They didn't ask in any sort of polite way; in fact another option was to get in each other's faces and demand that a teammate-- in Cam's words-- pass the fucking puck!

And yes, I was now calling him Cam.

My Cam. Although he didn't know that yet.

My character became more like him with every skate, and every game film we watched, and I only grew to admire Cam more each moment we were together. He wasn't captain of the Storm, that was Charlie with the big house, but Cameron was a leader on the team, and it was clear he was damn good at his job.

When he asked to talk after our latest practice-- one in which I'd skated the entire rink in reverse-- I never even thought it would be bad news.

"My brother's fiancée is having a dinner party this weekend for wedding stuff, and I have to attend so..." He hesitated, and I waited for him to ask me to go with him. He didn't. "We'll have to take a few days off from training."

Nothing. No invite. No introduction to his family. *Damn it.*

"Oh, hey that's fine." I said, using my best it's-all-cool tone. "You should for sure be with your family for that. I can keep working on my short stops. Spraying ice and all that. Looks great on camera." I knocked his arm, all buddy-buddy, and he smiled at me.

"It won't be for long," he apologized, "sorry to break up the training, but y'know, family is everything."

I smiled even harder. "I can manage. One more practice, and then, go be with family."

Take me with you.

Chapter 14

Cameron

THE NEXT DAY'S TRAINING WAS ALL OVER THE PLACE.

For me.

Finn was finding his stride with each session, and I was proud of his dedication to his craft. He'd worked hard to hone himself into a passable hockey player. Would he ever make the pros? Absolutely not. Was he good enough to play a pro on the silver screen? For sure. Feeling at a loss about taking Cam time—which was stupid because good mental health dictated having me time as well as we time—I had instituted a reward system for Finn.

Today, and today only... that was a lie because I planned to carry on with this reward system for as long as I could... every time he aced a move, he got a kiss.

There was no one here who would see. The lone security guys, Jed, and Todd, didn't bother with us at all. I wasn't sure if that was something that Atlas had set up or if Finn had asked for total privacy, but it worked for me.

Finn was glowing with pride after socking a puck into the net, a high shot over my rather weak glove hand—Philippe, I was not—and skated into my crease wearing a comically large pucker. I gave him a playful shove away from the blue paint, then fished out the puck with the goalie paddle I'd borrowed from the storage room.

"Leave my crease before I am made to come unhinged on your face," I snarled in my best Phillippe imitation.

Finn gaped, his face falling into a mournful expression that could win him an Oscar. "My heart... is broken," he gasped, clutching at his chest, then falling into my arms.

I grabbed, then held him up, no small feat as he was a big man, and shook free from my catcher.

Finn fell back over my arm in true movie starlet faux faint form, his long lashes fluttering as his body went limp. Down to the ice we went, him on top, which I was learning, was a position the man *really* liked, and laid in the net facing each other.

"You're a damn fool," I chuckled while he pushed up to sit on my well-padded groin. He removed my borrowed mask from my head, all playfulness gone as his gaze burst into flame. He took off his helmet and flung it over his shoulder. I vaguely heard it hit the boards.

"I'm a fool for you, Cam," he whispered, then spread himself over me and captured my mouth in a kiss that stole every rational thought I possessed. The temperature in the crease rose by about fifty degrees. How we weren't lying in a puddle was beyond me. I threaded a hand into his hair, loving the dampness of his exertion in the thick gold mass of curls. We were both so padded up that any kind of sensation was minimal, but jeez, I was aroused when the kiss ended. Getting a boner while wearing a couple of cups was not comfortable in the least.

"I'm going to miss this," I confessed, massaging his scalp just behind his ear. "I don't get to make out with someone during most of my practices with the team. Coach frowns on frottage on the ice." He smiled down at me, a lonely, soft smile that made me regret setting up this break. "I'm coming back. You know that right?"

"I know." He wanted to say more it seemed, but he didn't. Instead, he stole a fast kiss, pushed to his feet, and offered me his hand. Up I went as if I weighed nothing. We stood there in front of the net, both of us chewing on something, but neither daring to express whatever it was we were feeling. "Let's get a little more work in before you have to catch your flight home."

I nodded, picked up Phillippe's old mask, and pulled it down over my head.

Time for that game face, Cameron.

. . .

IT WAS GOOD TO BE BACK HOME IN SCOTTSDALE enjoying the serenity of a post-dinner cocktail on my parents' back deck.

I missed Finn, but I tried my hardest not to let it get in the way of my family time.

Kelly was beside me on a glider, Lyle and his lovely bride-to-be were sitting by the pool, swishing their naked toes in the water, and Mom and Dad were seated by the brick chimney sipping wine as Dad filled me in on life at the office. He was one of the top podiatrists in Scottsdale. Mom was a cosmetic dentist. To say they were well-off would be putting it mildly. But it hadn't always been this way.

There had been lean times when they were just getting started in an affluent neighborhood that didn't always take kindly to those of Mexican heritage. My mother's family was from Guadalupe, and my father's people from the United Kingdom. Mom liked to tease that at least two of her kids looked like the Escarra clan. Lyle, well, Lyle had the fair complexion that my father's side of the family also had. He claimed it set him apart from his siblings, then asked for the SPF ten thousand sunscreen. Kelly, Mom, and I were dark-haired with skin that tanned with very little of the burning that Dad and Lyle suffered through.

They were now very comfortable in life, and all of their kids were successful in their own careers. Life was good for them, and I always felt a calm when I came home.

"... unwrapped the bindings to check on his ulcers when I discovered—"

"Morty, please, must we discuss foot issues over wine?" Mom asked, interrupting my father's recounting of one Mr. Axel North, senator from the great state of Arizona, who at the age of ninety-two was having issues with his diabetic feet.

"You told Cameron about the porcelain veneers you did for the soda pop heiress," Dad argued, without any real vinegar.

"Yes, and that was to remind all of our children and their soon-to-be wives that soda pop is terrible for your teeth. Acidic drinks can eat through your veneers."

"Yes, Mama," the three of us said by rote.

I did my best to not overdo on soda or coffee, not just for my pretty white teeth, but for my waistline. I did indulge more than I should, but so far, the coffee and sugar hadn't gotten the better of me or my veneers. There were upsides to having a mom who fixed teeth for a living. So far, all of my veneers hadn't been tested by a puck, stick, or too many cups of caffeine. It was only a matter of time though...

"Personally, I think coffee is repugnant," Lyle called from the pool, his arms locked behind him, head tipped back to watch the stars blink to life overhead.

The backyard of my parents' home was landscaped to match the surroundings. Lots of cactus and native flowers in low, rocky gardens, a pool with a splashing waterfall, and a covered patio with imported tiles and stonework walls that complimented the outside fireplace. The inside of the house was airy, open, and very much influenced by our Spanish culture. As were many of the mansions in this neighborhood.

"Did you know naturally brewed herbal tea is full of antioxidants? Carmine brews us a pot of purple tea daily. Perhaps you two should try brewing your own teas instead of wasting money buying those silly foamy coffees out all the time. Fiscally speaking, paring down eating out will save you at least a thousand dollars a year, which you could then invest in a solid IRA that will make your financial advisor proud."

Kelly and I rolled our eyes. "Lyle, I don't have a financial advisor, but if I did, I would tell him he had a better chance of seeing Jesus Christ than he did of prying my coconut milk iced macchiato out of my hands."

Carmine laughed. Lyle sighed at his fiancée, as only a banker faced with a sister who liked frivolous coffee expenditures could.

"Since I can't talk feet, I'm going to go sit with the girls. Cameron, it's b*eeeee*n a while since you visited the hives," Dad said, pleased at his bee pun.

I gave my little sister a peck on her smooth cheek, rose, and joined my father for a slow walk to the hives. Mom and Carmine started talking wedding, which brought Kelly into the conversation as she was the maid of honor. Carmine had claimed Kelly as her sister and me as her twin brother as we were the same age. She had no siblings, and her parents had died young, which was why my father was walking her down the aisle next year. We all adored Carmine. What she saw in Lyle was a mystery for the ages. Love is blind, as they say.

Whoever *they* were.

I wondered what they would say if they could witness the mess that I'd stumbled into. What words of sage advice would the mysterious *they* pass along to a soul who had shunned any kind of relationship, and now, without warning and one smile at a time, was balancing on the edge of a ravine as deep as the Grand Canyon.

"… how full the frames are. I'll be putting the supers on the hives within the next two weeks."

"Uh-huh," I replied as my sight lingered on the setting sun. The western part of the yard was alive with flowering plants and honeybees making one last journey out to collect pollen before calling it a day. It had been a day of packing as fast as I could, then jumping on the first available flight to get me out of LA. Even being a state away didn't seem to be helping though. I could still see Finn's eyes in the dark blues of the evening sky.

I wish I'd asked him to come with me.

"Of course, if that were to happen, then your mother and I would have to sprout wings and grow stingers."

My mind was on Finn, as always, as I wondered what he was doing tonight. I'd sent one fast text when I had arrived, but that was it. I wanted to send more though, and that was the whole problem in one big, closeted nutshell.

"I've always thought about what it might be like to sting the neighbor's wife. She has enormous pollen baskets."

"Yeah, me too." Then what he said sank in, and I threw my father a befuddled and shocked glance. *"What did you just say about Mrs. Wilcox?"*

"Ah, there you are!" he joked, giving me a soft nudge in the side as we took our seats in the two Adirondack chairs Dad had put out in this massive, and busy, flower garden. "I knew if I kept talking you'd drift back to the conversation in time."

"I'm sorry, Dad." I shoved my fingers into my hair as I exhaled though my mouth.

"That was quite the sigh. Want to tell me what's weighing on you so heavily?" Dad leaned up, resting his elbows on his knees, his gray eyes locked on me. "Is it the finals loss?"

"Sort of, sure, I'm disappointed that we lost. We were so close."

"Well, that is tough. But you've been through hard losses before, Son. If you can look back objectively and learn from the mistakes that were made, then that loss will have served a purpose."

He was right. I would move past the loss. I'd started

to already, as had most of the team. It still hurt, sure, but the sharp pain had lessened. Dad had been through a ton of highs and lows with me as I'd gone through the various age brackets of youth hockey right through my collegiate career. Hell, even into the pros. Being an athlete was all about learning how to cull whatever knowledge you could from a brutal loss and applying it to your next time on the ice or field.

"Is there something else, Cameron? You seem abnormally distant tonight," Dad questioned softly, reaching out to lay a hand on my knee. "You know you can talk to me, or your mom, about anything."

I knew that. Truly, I did, but this was just... How did I even begin to say what I was feeling when I was so scared of saying what I was feeling? I felt like a dog chasing its tail, spinning in circles while getting dizzier and dizzier.

"There's this guy," I chanced, glancing at my father.

He'd been very accepting of my sexuality when I'd come out in college. As had Mom and Lyle and Kelly. But this was different. This was me getting snared. No, that wasn't the right sentiment. Finn hadn't set a trap for me. Shit, he was as wound up in the choking wire that had us both by the neck as I was.

"Did he hurt you?" Dad asked, then gave my knee a squeeze. I shook my head, unable to conjure up the words so that they could make sense. "Did he steal your heart?"

I nodded. The rush of emotion felt like a dam

breaking. The story of Cam and Finn flowed from me like honey, only this was far stickier, but God, loving Finn was just as sweet. And I thought that I did love him, or felt something powerful for the man, which had me jabbering nonstop about every drab damn detail of the situation we were in. Dad said little, nodded, uhm-hummed, and patted my knee while I word-vomited all over his pretty bee garden. When I reached the part where I got on a plane and flew home, I was spent. Exhausted. Like I'd been made to do speed sprints or a bag skate. My spine met the back of the chair, my eyes drifted shut, and I did my best to pull myself back together.

"Sounds to me like you've fallen pretty hard, Cam," Dad said as a bee flew past my ear. I cracked one eye to make sure she had continued on her way to the hive, then stared out at the mesa and the purple-pink mounds of stone that had sat there for thousands of years. "Does he feel the same way about you?"

I shrugged. "I don't know. We agreed this would be just friends. There was an NDA."

"I have lots of friends, but I don't jump them in the bathroom and get jiggy with it with them. I save that for your mother." I scrunched my face. Did any child ever want to hear about his parents getting jiggy with it? No, they did not. Still, I appreciated the input. "Perhaps you need to explain your feelings to him. Maybe he's in the same boat. Sometimes things start out as one thing, then they grow into a different thing. I'm using thing a lot."

"It's fine. This isn't English class. Say thing ten times in each sentence, I don't care. I'm just… this has felt… good. I'm so scared, Dad. I've done my best to avoid any kind of emotional entanglements, yet here I am, entangled but good."

"I'm not sure where you ever got the idea that being alone is how to face the world. Just look at the bees." He released my knee to throw his hands open to the honey bees returning to the brightly painted boxes. "They know the value of being one of many."

"They're Borg, clearly."

He snorted. "Very funny. The point I was trying to make was that no creature does well alone."

"I wasn't alone, or lonely."

"Having a stranger in your bed and sharing your soul with another person are two very different things. And while you can get pleasure from a purely sexual experience, I've found that loving someone openly is more sexually stimulating than the other."

"But see that's just it. We can't be openly anything. I just…" I raked my fingers through my hair as a shooting star raced across the desert sky. "It's not at all how I thought love would be. If it even is love."

"Oh, I'm pretty sure it is. And by the sounds, it's exactly how love feels for all of us. Like stepping out of a plane with no parachute."

"Yes, God, yes, it feels like that only a million times

scarier. I don't know what to do, or if there is even any point of exploring how I feel when it won't go anywhere. It's just..." I let it dangle. What more was there for me to say? "Should I tell him?" I asked on the weakest of whispers.

"I think you should, yes. Give the man the chance to say it back."

"What if he doesn't?"

"What if he does?"

Yeah, that was the question.

Either way he replied was a field filled with sharp stakes and tiger traps.

Gee, love was grand.

Not.

Chapter 15

Finn

It had only been three days.

It felt like a lot longer.

I'd kept up my practice, the rink emptied of everyone except me and security at the front desk. I'd made friends with Jed and Todd, who seemed to be on duty all the time, and who never worried me or fussed over me or asked me questions.

I wished they'd talk to me instead of staring at various screens.

Because my thoughts were too much, too knotted, too… everything, and I was lonely and veering toward pathetic. I skated the length of the rink crossovers, switching direction, smooth, and then angled my skates to come to a fancy stop, sending ice into the net.

"He scores!" I yelled, balling my fists, and reaching for the sky with my mouth wide open.

Nope that didn't work, particularly when raising

180

said hands put me so much off-balance I ended up ass over tail into the bench area.

I tried again, skating for the net, icing, and this time in celebration of my imaginary scoring, I shot an imaginary arrow using the stick as the bow.

Nope. That wasn't the character.

Also, yet again I ended up in the bench.

Maybe I should stick to a celebration the same as Cameron's, which was a firm nod and a chef's kiss to the crowd. I could do that.

I spent so long deciding which hand to do the kiss with that, when I managed it, I punched myself in the face with the bulky gloves.

Finesse is not my friend.

"Mr. Kerrigan? Sir?"

I skated over to where both Jed and Todd were escorting in a mountain in human form. A mountain who winked at me, and then returned my grin. Company at last.

"This man says he has permission to be here," Jed said with a sniff.

"I am Philippe Jacques Andre Pageau. I am team special puck holder. Of course, I should be here," the man said in heavily accented French.

"That's Phillipe!" I exclaimed, coming to a sudden stop when my belly met the rink surround. It was Phillipe who reached over and caught me, shaking his head when I clung to him for dear life.

He let out a stream of words, and I could only make

out one of them—Cameron—and from Phillipe's expression, he wasn't impressed with my landing in his arms.

"He didn't have a pass." Todd laid his hand on Phillipe's arm, which the big goalie soon shrugged away. To my knowledge, there were passes for a skeleton staff, and one the security company had made Cam wear and sign the back of. I didn't think anyone else would want to visit, and Cam and I had been in our own bubble with the staff mostly staying in the office side of the building with a promise that the ice time was to remain private. I'd paid a ton of money for privacy, and so far, no one had caused any issues. But seeing Phillipe was a breath of fresh air.

"Add him to the list. Let him in." It would be nice to have the company, although how he'd known to come here was up for debate.

"There is no official list, sir," Jed said.

"There is now. Add Phillipe to it."

Jed and Todd both narrowed their eyes at me, and I sighed. It was Atlas who paid them, Atlas who hadn't thought to make a list beyond the staff here, but it was me who paid Atlas.

"It's okay, guys. He's a friend."

They muttered together, and Phillipe took the distraction and stepped away from them, a huge bag slipping from his back.

"We skate. We talk about heartache," he said, and that didn't sound ominous at all.

He vanished down the tunnel—I assumed to change —and Todd elected to sit in the stands, close enough to watch me, while Jed went back to reception. Boy, they were taking this looking out for me very seriously, but I didn't want an audience of anyone, particularly not stony-faced Todd.

I clumped after Phillipe, ignoring the glimpse of his ass, and yanking out my phone. One short message to Atlas later, I headed back out to find Todd taking a call, then moving away with one more pointed stare at Phillipe, who was by the tunnel waiting to come out on the ice. He wasn't wearing his goalie stuff, but he was in Storm purple, skates on, and a hockey stick at his side. He waited until Todd had disappeared, then lifted his face to the rafters and inhaled deeply. More French —I needed to learn more of the language of love—and then he skated lazy circles, forward, backward, and arrived at my side with a broad grin.

"Skate first, heart things after," he announced, and then shoved me.

If I'd been expecting it, then maybe I could have stayed on my skates, as it was, I sprawled on the ice and stared up at Phillipe, who laughed.

Who was I kidding—even if I had been expecting the push, I would still have ended up on my ass.

He helped me up and bro-hugged me, then set me away from him and pointed at my knees. "Bend them!" he ordered. I rolled my eyes at him, and for a second, he gave me a death glare, and I waited for a torrent of

French-Canadian abuse. Instead, he snorted another laugh and pulled me back for another hug. "Skate!"

So, we skated, we circled the rink, we shoved at each other, we shot at goal, and he told me to bend my knees twenty-three times—I know because I counted, and it broke Cam's record of seventeen.

Then, we stopped. I was exhausted—gassed, to use the official term—and followed Phillipe down the tunnel to the locker rooms. Were we going to talk now? No, it seemed, because Phillipe stripped down and headed for the showers, with me close after.

When I was toweling my hair, he stared at me, and I wondered who was going to start this heart talk he seemed to be so desperate for.

"Don't break Cameron's heart," he warned out of nowhere. "He's a good man. A fine man with a heart that feels..." He paused, searching for a word. "Big things."

"What are you're talking about," I prevaricated. Had Cam told Phillipe about us? Had he told the whole team? Did everyone out there on Instagram know about what we were doing?

"He said nothing," Phillipe interrupted my stupid-ass imagination. "But we see things."

"'We'?" I asked weakly.

"The team. Cam'ron is our..." Again, he was searching. "Grand gâteau." He frowned. "Non. Ce n'est pas un gâteau; c'est un grand cœur. Ummm, au milieu de l'équipe. Giant sweetheart for Storm."

I nodded because I assumed he'd just summarized in accented English what he'd said in French. I could read between the lines—Cameron was the heart of the team, a big part, and his friend was worried I was going to hurt him.

I wouldn't do that.

I missed him.

I wanted to be with him—I wanted to meet his family and earn their friendship. I wanted everyone to see how I felt about him.

"He could have anyone," Phillipe murmured, and I leaned forward to hear him better. "But I see things, and I can see he could love you. Take care of him. Oui?"

Phillipe was up and gone before I could process what he'd said. Cam could love me. Was it outside the realm of possibility that maybe he felt the same way about me as I did him? Could I have fallen in love in just a few weeks? Or was it the freedom of allowing myself to have this with him? Was I drunk on the possibilities?

What would I be like if he wasn't in my life anymore?

Would I be okay with that?

No. I wanted more; I wanted Cam for as long as I could imagine.

So maybe this was the start of love, the seed of something more.

After all, why not? When the time is right, the heart knows.

This new love was an enormous pressure in my chest that made me want to tell the world I was with Cameron Chavkin, and to do it now.

Yeah.

Love.

What about my part in *The Cup*? What about my career? What about not being hired for parts because of who I slept with? What about Cameron and his testosterone-laced team?

The what-abouts were killing me.

THE CAR SERVICE TOOK ME FROM THE RINK DIRECTLY TO the studio, and once dropped off I headed up to the labyrinth of rooms on the fifth floor. From the window, the entirety of Hollywood lay out in all directions, a community of story tellers that loved their work. I was at home here. I belonged here.

I loved Cam.

I wanted it all.

Was that wrong?

"Okay, everyone?" River Grierson rapped his knuckles on the table, but it wasn't for everyone else's benefit, it was for me, because what with love and my ever-present battling thoughts, plus trying to channel the character of Hayden "Mac" McKenzie, I was a mess. I focused in on River, who narrowed his eyes at me, and I could almost read the expression he had as *stop-fucking-up-or-you're-fired*.

He cleared his throat. "Okay then, from the top of page seventeen; our hero, Mac, is at home, coming to terms with the loss of the Cup, and go!"

I read my lines, wondering if this was how Cam would say them, wondering what Cam was doing right now. Was he missing me?

"Okay, everyone, let's call it a day. Finn, can you stay back please?"

Everyone else scuttled out of the room, a couple of them glancing back at me and offering me sympathetic half-smiles.

When the last of them had left, River shut the door and scooted a chair close to mine.

"Talk to me," he urged.

"Sorry, my head isn't right today."

"Tell me what is stopping you from feeling the character—do I need to get the writer in and—"

"No, this is all on me."

He patted my knee and then, sat back. "Talk to me if you like."

"I want this role."

He nodded. "And there is nothing you can tell me that will change that. Unless you've killed someone, have you killed someone?"

"No, jeez. No. It's just…"

"There's no 'just' here, and this is a safe place." He waved at the desk in the corner of his vast office space, and for the first time I noticed the strategically positioned rainbows, and a photo of River with another man. Everything seemed to add up in that moment—River Grierson was queer? Or at least, an ally? How did I not know that? Why did he come to think I needed a safe space? Was I doing the subterfuge wrong? Was I messing this up?

"I can't skate," I blurted, and his eyes widened. Maybe I shouldn't have opened with that. "I mean I can now. I've been having lessons from Cam, Cameron Chavkin, from the LA Storm, and I can do all the shots you need, but I fell in love with him, and I'm not out and I want to be, but then who will take me seriously because I'm just some half-assed action hero with stupid quippy one-liners and an acting start in daytime soaps. You say this is a safe space, but what if the studio pulls funding, what if…" I couldn't carry on.

He chuckled, and that seemed so wrong. "I *am* the studio. It's all mine. I've reinvested every single cent I've made back into this place. You want to come out, you do that. I don't have time for any place that forces a person to hide their true self."

"You don't?"

"Nope. You don't have many chances to find love in this world, so do what I did, tell the man you love him, then cling to him until he believes you. Acting is your job, but Cameron…"

"He's my heart."

"Exactly. Now, tell the man you love him. Grab that love and don't let go. Then, tell the world if you want to, or don't, but either way, you're playing the role of

Mac, and I want you back here two p.m. tomorrow sharp, for another run-through, and this time with a clear head."

I COULDN'T SLEEP, COULDN'T EVEN LOOK AT MY PHONE, even though I saw the first message was from Cam explaining he might be a bit late in the morning.

If I started talking to him now, I'd probably lose my shit and ruin everything.

River was right; acting might be my career, but Cam was my heart.

I was dressed and waiting by the ice when he appeared, and I was going to play this cool and not leap at him, but he kissed me -- long, slow, drugging kisses that made me cling to him.

It had to be now.

I had to tell him, throw the dice, and see how they fell. "We need to talk."

Chapter 16

Cameron

Well, that was always ominous.

It felt really bad to be on this end of those four famous words.

I'd not been dumped before. Never. Simply because I always hit the bricks before anyone could form an attachment. Now, I knew why I'd booked after each hookup. This feeling sucked.

"Sure, yeah, we can talk," I replied trying to sound as cool as possible on the outside. Inside, I could feel my heart cracking. *Damn it.* I should have stuck to my guns and not allowed myself to fall for this man. Everyone knew you didn't skate when the weather turned warm, and the ice got thin. This was why. Now, I had to sit down on the home bench, smile, and pretend that him saying we had to call it quits was hunky and fucking dory with me. "Let's sit."

He nodded, his hair glowing like ingots under the

rather harsh lights of the rink. Every push to the bench felt like a step to the gallows.

We went over the boards, just as I had taught him, and settled down on the cold, hard bench. I placed my stick over my lap, worked up all the intestinal fortitude that I had, and looked his way. Both of us had removed our skates, then tied our sneakers. Yes, I was stalling. Big. Time.

He smiled at me. A soft, fluffy kind of tender uplifting of his sweet lips that didn't sit right with what he was about to do. Was it proper protocol to dump someone while smiling at them? That seemed cruel.

"So, I had some time to think."

"Uh-huh." I began fiddling with the tape on my stick. Scraping a nail along the edge until I got a corner loose, then picked at it as I stared at Finn. "Thinking is good."

"Yeah, for sure. It's also pretty scary when you're thinking of big stuff."

Shit. Yep, here it came. This was when he was going to explain that he enjoyed our side benefits, but it was time to call it quits. After all, he needed to focus on the movie, I could feel it. He'd learned quickly and there wasn't much more for me to teach him. His skating was good enough for a movie—and his checking skills were much improved. My ass could testify to that, as he'd knocked me to my rump during a heated scrabble over the puck in the corner. Afterwards, he had kissed it better. Then fucked it better. Damn it. I was going to miss his kisses...

"... had to really go through some stuff to get to the realization that I am stupid in love with you."

It took a moment for the words to soak into my medulla or frontal lobe or whatever part of the brain dealt with wild emotional shit.

"You what?" I asked because my head was still back on the ass-kissing for some reason. "I didn't hear you because I was recalling how well you dicked me."

He grinned the grin of a man who knew he had fucked his man well and thoroughly. "Yeah, I did dick you pretty damn well."

"You said you love me," I said, the sticky underbelly of my tape had left my fingers tacky. "Did I hear you say that?"

"You did. I said it. Are you freaking out? You look like you're freaking out." He bit down on his lower lip, big blue eyes filled with horror, fingers gripping the edge of his jersey.

"I'm not... no, not freaking out. Well, sort of, but not because you said you... love me." He looked dubious. I gently removed his hands from the hem of his sweater. They were cold, so I lifted them to my lips. I placed tiny pecks to his scabby knuckles. Knuckles marked up like a real hockey player. He'd come so far. I loved him so much. If I had been standing my knees would be knocking, I was shaking so hard. "I'm... I was sure you were going to tell me to hit the freeway." His eyebrows beetled. "I thought you were done with me. Our lessons are about over. I assumed you were going to break up with me."

"Are we in a place where we *can* break up?" His question was earnest.

I shrugged before lowering his hands, my fingers sliding between his. "I don't know. To be honest, Finn, I don't know jack shit about relationships. All I know is that the thought of never seeing you again makes me queasy and scared. More scared than being hurt. That's what love is, right?"

"Sure, in a way. Do you want more from us than this?"

"Fuck, yes. I want lots more."

He smiled in relief. My mouth found his. The kiss was explosive, gentle yes, but so filled with raw emotion. I pulled back after a moment, to rest my nose alongside his, as we battled to catch our breaths.

"Oh good. I do too. I want lots more. I want... I think I want to come out," he whispered.

Wow. Oh, shit. That was... Massive. I pulled back even more, sitting straight now, my sight combing his face for any signs of anxiety. I saw a little.

"Finn, that's a huge step. You don't have to come out. I'm willing to wait for you to find the right time."

He frowned a bit. "That's just it. When will it ever be the right time?"

Okay, he had me there. "But your career will take a hit."

"Probably, but maybe not. I don't care, honestly, Cam; I'm *so* tired of living my life in constant fear. I want to be able to touch you in public. I want to not have to hide in my house or yours just so we can kiss. I want to tell the world that you're mine… if you want to be mine?"

I kissed him with all the whirling emotions inside me. Our tongues tangled as our fingers tightened around each other's, the world melting away to a chilly blur around us. Nothing else mattered but this moment.

"God, I do love you," I croaked, my throat tight with feelings I wasn't sure how to express. "Emoting isn't my thing, it's yours, but I am crazy about you. It feels like someone elbowed me in the head every time I look at you."

He chortled a bit, his lips a mere inch from mine— his breath sweet from the coffee we'd stopped to buy on the way in—so close.

"You romantic fool," he teased, stealing another kiss, then leaning in close to rest his brow on my shoulder. I dropped a kiss to his hair, my dopey gaze flitting around the rink. A flash of something purple caught my eye by the northern exit.

"Shit," I snapped, rising to my skates to watch a small figure in one of my damn Storm jerseys booking ass. "We've been made."

Finn's rosy cheeks went ashen. How had anyone gotten past Jed and Todd? I took off, climbing up and over the railing that ran across the tunnel that leads from the benches to the locker rooms. Finn fell in behind me as I locked eyes on the frame of a kid. Black hair, tan skin, about thirteen or so, maybe, just judging by his gangly build. The kid was faster, but I had longer legs. I also had reach. I caught him and pulled him into me gently. Finn clambered over the plastic benches, reaching us a moment after I had captured our quarry.

"Hand it over," Finn said, his breathing barely hitched. The man was in phenomenal shape. The kid, who now sounded like he was crying, held up his cellphone. "Unlock it," Finn said—God, he sounded sad —and the kid did as he was asked. I loosened my hold on him but didn't let go entirely. This was not the way I liked to interact with fans, but my faith in this kid was hurt badly when Finn showed me the shots of us kissing.

"Little dude, that was so uncool," I said to the child resting loosely against me. I wasn't so much holding him, as he was seeking comfort from me.

"I know… I'm… I'm…" The boy began to really cry now. Big, choking sobs that made me feel like a first-class jerk. Finn spent a moment deleting the images of us, then gestured for the boy to sit down. I steered him to the top row of benches, then let go. The kid sat with a sniffle, then pulled his sleeve under his running nose. Gross. But hey, I did that on the ice when it was necessary, so I didn't chide him.

"What's your name?" I asked of the little guy.

He glanced up at me with big brown eyes. "Manuel," he replied shakily. I glanced at Finn, who had taken a seat on Manuel's left. I dropped down beside the boy.

"Okay, Manuel, want to tell us why you were sneaking around in here?"

He glanced at me, then Finn, sniveled a bit more, and then gave his nose one more wipe.

"I saw your car outside," Manuel replied, his tears slowing. "I came in the service door, there's no cameras there, and I'm your biggest fan," he said, his gaze meeting mine.

"Thanks, but, seriously, my man, what you did there was uncool." I jerked my chin to his phone as it dangled from his fingers.

"I know. I'm sorry. I just..." He drew in a huge breath, then let it out in one massive snotty exhale. Finn fished a hankie out of his back pocket and passed it over to the lad. After a big blow, Manuel tried to return the hankie, but Finn told him to keep it. I would have made the same call. "I wanted to show it to my dad. I swear that was all! I wouldn't have sold it to any papers or put it online. I just wanted my dad to see that guys who are gay are tough too."

Oh. "Are you hiding something from your father, Manuel?" I asked in Spanish.

He replied with a sluggish nod, then began telling me about his life. He lived near the rink, hell, he was even on one of the teams in CC's Club. He began rambling on about how he felt different from the other kids in school, but how his father was a tough guy, real macho, which was common among Latino men. It had taken my Mexican uncles and male cousins some adjusting to accept me, but they had, mostly. The ones who didn't could go sit in a fucking ditch. But I got his story and his struggle. As did Finn, who was staring at me in confusion.

Jed and Todd arrived--too little, too late-- and I shot them an angry glance. They both stepped closer as if they were going to get involved. "You can go," I said. Then, I turned back to Manuel. "Hey, we best speak in English. My man's Spanish sucks." I jerked a thumb at Finn, who had the good grace to nod. It felt nice to call him mine. Aloud and all that.

"It really does. I had to have all my lines in a Spanish shampoo commercial that I did a few years back dubbed in," Finn confessed. That made Manuel throw him a weak smile.

"So, your dad..." I prompted.

"Yeah, he loves the Storm. Beer every game, lots of chest-pounding and all that, you know. He thinks you're super cool," he said as he stared at me. "I thought... I don't know... that he might be okay with me being gay, if he saw that tough guys were too."

No shit, this was crazy heavy.

Finn looked about ready to weep. "Is this what it's come to?" he asked after a moment or two of silence had passed. "Are we now chasing down kids and demanding they keep my secret?"

I had no answer for that. Yeah, I guess that was what it had come down to for sure. That felt pretty rotten.

"I'm really sorry. I know I shouldn't have taken your picture," Manuel murmured. I ruffled his hair as I studied Finn for signs of what the hell to do now.

"It's fine. We totally get it. We've both been there," Finn announced to the world, which made me gape. Finn glanced at me. I nodded. "Guess I just came out though, huh?"

"Guess so, baby," I replied. Manuel sat there between us, his dark eyes darting from Finn to me, as if he had never witnessed two men staring lovingly at each other. "You know, maybe if we visited with you and your dad, and had a talk with him he'd be okay with hearing you out, Manuel." The boy's jaw went slack. He nodded and blinked as if words had failed him. "Cool, let's take a walk." I rose, offered Finn my hand, and he clasped it. And he did not let go the whole time we strolled to Manuel's home four blocks away.

It was a lovely home in a heavily Latino section of town. Modest, but well-taken care of, lots of love in the house. You could sense it the moment you entered. The smells of lunch being made lured us into the small kitchen where three adults—a woman of about forty, a man about the same age, and an older woman of about sixty or so—glanced up at us as we entered. The older woman at the stove preparing what smelled like some ten-alarm chili, dropped the spoon she was stirring the meat with into the large pot.

It took a few minutes to get everyone calmed down and answer most of their questions. Finn and I learned that the family was compromised of Manuel, his grandmother, Teresa; her son, Lorenzo; and his wife, Maria. Teresa insisted we dine with them, so we ate lunch at that small, scarred table that had come all the way from Taxco with Teresa and her husband forty years ago. Finn dove into the chili with gusto, only to break into a sweat so severe we all worried he might pass out. Teresa's chili was not for those with tender tummies. After a few glasses of milk for my man—that sounded so damn good—we moved outside where it was cooler. The backyard was small, packed full of flowers and pottery that Maria made in her studio.

Lorenzo offered us some beer, which we politely refused, citing our athlete/actor status. He laughed, then sat in a chair in the shade of a rollout sunshade.

Teresa brought out some iced tea for us, and then, possibly sensing something big was brewing with the males, went back inside. The soft feminine sounds of the two women speaking in Spanish drifted out an older jalousie window. It reminded me of home here in some ways. Yes, my parents had more disposable income, but the sounds of a loving family were the same no matter how many zeroes one had in their checking accounts.

Manuel glanced at me after several moments spent talking about sports rolled past.

I cleared my throat, looked right at Lorenzo—a handsome man with thick dark hair and a fashionable goatee—who met my gaze with slight confusion.

"Your son would like to tell you something," I said as an opener, before I shifted my attention to Manuel.

The lad fell in on himself for a moment, the weight of what he wished to say a heavy one, but one slow word at a time, he told his father his story. Lorenzo's attention whipped back and forth from his son to me, now sitting with my hand on Finn's knee in an open and possessive way. I hoped to be able to touch him all the time as soon as we figured out how to proceed. But for now, this was enough.

The women grew silent indoors as Manuel talked. His father, a proud man, began to tear up when his son told him that he feared he wouldn't love him if he knew he were gay. Then, thank all the gods, Lorenzo opened his arms for Manuel. Finn's lower lip wobbled as father and son hugged it out, and even though this was not our moment, I felt a large part of it. Sitting back, trying to be unobtrusive, we smiled at each other when Manuel's mother and grandmother came through the back door to join in on the hugs.

Sensing it was our time to leave, we stood, thanked them for the food and drink, and slipped out of the front after leaving one of my business cards on the kitchen table. The family would be my guest at the Storm Pride night next season.

Stepping out into the bright LA sun, I glanced over at Finn. He looked as if he were ascending to the heavens his glow was that bright.

"That was amazing," he said as a bike delivery guy rubbernecked as he passed by, almost running into the back of a sanitation truck idling at a red light. "I can make a difference, Cam. *Together, we* can make a difference."

"Yeah, baby, we can."

I held out my hand, and he took it. We walked back to my car discussing our plans for our future. I liked the word *our* quite a bit. I planned to use it often from this point onward.

Chapter 17

Finn

"Ready?" Atlas asked for the tenth time. My statement had been ready an hour ago, but lawyers calling in, keen to avoid any negative implications for the *Rapid* movies, had demanded to sign off on everything I said. I'd wanted to tell them to go fuck themselves, but refrained given the way Atlas made a slicing motion across his neck as their demands echoed over the phone speaker.

"As ready as I'll ever be."

The statement was going live on all my social media, on the studio socials, plus more importantly, it was going to be backed up by Byrnes-Rose and the teams on the *Rapid* movies, plus River Grierson and his team on *The Cup* production. It spoke about courage and authenticity, but my courage was more like manic fear. I couldn't stop tapping my fingers on my knees, I couldn't sit still, the room was too warm, then too cold, the sun too bright, then thunder clouds too dark. In the first draft, Atlas had used words such as talent, charisma, and dedication, but I'd nixed them all. No one wanted to have to *appreciate the newfound understanding of my authentic self,* nor that my statement *came after a period of self-reflection and personal growth.* I wanted it to be simple. I wanted to add my love for my family and my friends, and I wanted it done.

"Cameron?" Atlas asked, as Cameron took my hand and laced our fingers. He'd wanted to add a line about our new relationship, and even though I wanted any fallout to be just on me, I agreed. Seems like this really was love because I wanted his name entwined with mine forever.

"It's okay, Finn." Cameron squeezed my fingers.

"It should feel better than this," I murmured. "It's what I want, so why am I so nervous."

"What's the worst that can happen?" he asked, and I wished I didn't have a huge list of worries. "Your family loves you; I love you, and I'm not going anywhere."

"I was going to wait until after *The Cup* was released," I said once more, just to hear the words.

"You can still pull the statement," Cam said, and leaned his head on my shoulder. "Doesn't change a thing between us, or with whatever understanding you have with River Grierson and his new movie."

"But it could change things for kids, ones like Manuel."

"Yeah."

I nodded at Atlas. "Do it."

He pressed a button to begin the process, and that was it.

I was out in Hollywood.

And I had a hockey player for a boyfriend.

COMING OUT WAS A MASS OF PUBLIC STATEMENTS, private messages, family support, expressions of support and love, but along with it came the hate. A lot of hate.

Some of the worst was online, and I chose not to look at it after the first twenty or so comments, which were irrational and cruel. Other vitriol came by letter to the makers of the *Rapid* franchise—accusing the studio of leading people astray thinking that I could even play a hero when I was queer.

Like a gay man couldn't be a swashbuckling archaeologist with a psychic sidekick.

Whatever.

The news was met with overwhelming support from many, but the hate was enough that it burrowed into my thoughts, one conflicting nest of yuck. The sense of relief and freedom after sharing my statement was filled with the hope that coming out could inspire and empower others who may be going through similar experiences. However, no more than ten minutes after the statement went live the magnitude of the attention and expectations was big. It was as if the entire world had something to say about who I was and scrutinized every step I'd ever taken. The heaviness of responsibility as a potential role model fell like one of those ACME ten-ton weights on my shoulders, and I went from hope to concern in the first day, and straight on through to fear.

The threats were real.

Jed and Todd were now a permanent addition to my life, and whereas before I could get around with a car, now I was facing paparazzi at my gate, and worse, they were messing with Cam's life as well.

There were mixed reactions from the public, despite the majority being supportive. Many were cool with what I'd done, some even saying I was brave, and it was wrong to be labeled as brave just for wanting to be myself. Then, there were those who criticized me. I even drew the attention of a couple of church groups who had an awful lot of hate-filled rhetoric to throw at me and threatened to hold demonstrations at all my movies. I could handle criticism, after all I was a himbo in three made-to-sell movies, so I'd had my fair share of shit thrown at me, but when they'd started in on Cam, that was wrong. The negative comments and judgment I'd encountered moved on to judging Cam with LA Storm hockey forums pushing the blame on me being with him as the reason they lost the Stanley Cup.

Never mind we weren't even together then.

Fuckers.

In less than forty-eight hours, I went from thinking I was doing the right thing to questioning my decision to come out publicly at all.

It all started when, the morning after the news broke, a man with a camera climbed my gate. He jumped my fucking wall and sauntered up my driveway.

He didn't get far, Jed dealt with him, but at the same time, he and Todd declared my house unprotectable, unsafe, and probably open to snipers and camera operators alike.

Snipers? For fuck's sake, I'm gay, not a terrorist.

I might not have liked the place I lived in much, but it was the first thing I'd bought with my *Rapid* money, and it meant something. It freaking hurt to give in to the fear and pack my bags to leave, but that was what I had to do, according to Atlas, who'd booked me a suite in a hotel. He said it was fancy and big and luxurious, and all the other buzz words he thought might help the transition.

None of them did.

I didn't want fancy, big, and luxurious. I wanted safe and happy.

"What about my fish?" I asked Jed, and he exchanged glances with Todd, who shrugged. "I'm not leaving my fish to die! I won't let you leave them!" I shouted in Jed's face, and while he didn't react to indicate the level of rude I'd descended to, I was immediately sorry, and I apologized so much that Jed had to ask me to stop.

I couldn't believe I lost my shit like that with the poor guy.

"Atlas said something about having them moved to his office," Jed explained after I'd stopped apologizing. "He suggested we should get a bucket and—"

"You're not moving Fred and Wilma in a fucking bucket!" I yelled again.

What am I doing?

"Hey." Someone pulled me into a hug—Cam was here, and he was holding me as if I was made of glass, as if I could be broken.

"My fish," I blurted, and then buried my face in Cam's neck. "I don't want them to go with Atlas—he can't even look after plastic plants!"

"Okay, it's okay," Cam soothed.

I heard him and Jed chatting over my head, something about finding a fish expert with the aim of moving them to his place.

"You're taking my fish?" I sounded watery, and my chest was tight. "Will you remember to feed them, but not too much, and the oxygen levels need to be right. Will you—"

"Not just your fish." He kissed the tip of my nose. "I'm taking you home as well."

I stumbled back. "No."

He frowned. "No?"

"I can't ask you to do that. The paps will stand outside and make you miserable, people will fly drones over your house—and none of this is your fault." I scrubbed at my eyes, and then left my hands there, feeling way out of control.

"Can we have a moment, guys?" Footsteps on the marble floor indicated Jed and Todd had left us alone. "Look at me, sweetheart," he asked, and after a sniff I did. His eyes were dark with emotion, and bright, as if he was close to tears, or injustice was making him angry. I couldn't tell. All I know was that he was there by my side, and he was my everything. "Come home with me."

"I thought about going home to my parents, but it's not fair on them—"

"Move in with me."

"And my sister has the kids, and she's pregnant—"

"Move in with me," he repeated, insistent and so damn caring.

"I can't. It's better if I give you space. Atlas has a suite for me at the—"

"Let me rephrase this. Please come home with me. I love you. I'll look after you."

Nerves coiled inside me on top of anxiety, and it was all too much. "What if we can't separate our personal and professional lives? What if we have no privacy, what if coming out is more newsworthy than my acting or your hockey career? Jesus, Cam, they're saying dreadful things about you. Like it's your fault you lost because you were too busy fucking the Ken-Doll who pretends to be an actor. I don't even look like

Ken! Not to mention the things that they're saying about the rest of the team. Shit. I'm so sorry. Are they angry with me? Do they hate me?" Pain knifed into me at the thought of all those people at the party having targets on their back because of me.

He cupped my chin and nodded. "It's nothing we haven't heard before, okay? When the Storm lose, we've had our fair share of slurs thrown at us, saying we're weak because a few of us are open about who we might want to love, accusing me and some of the other guys of orgies in the locker room. Then, the next game we win, and suddenly, we're gods among men. Look, babe, it's just words, and what's important is you and me. So, please come to my place so we can work through this—"

"I can't—"

"Yes, you can. Please." Cam was so focused, gripping my upper arms, almost willing me to say yes.

"Someone got over my gate, Cam. They could have…" Hurt me, hated me, I didn't know.

"The security around my place is insane, it has to be with the number of idiots who try to get close to Rottie next door. Say yes, Finn."

"You really want me to—"

"Move in with me?" he pleaded. "And not just on a temporary basis. I know it's quick, and maybe we would have danced around the subject for months, but, fuck, I love you, and my place is a home you'd fit right into."

"I love you too." Not that it was the point of what he was saying, but it was worth repeating.

"We can get anything important you have here moved over."

I blinked at him. "I don't have anything important apart from Fred and Wilma."

He glanced around. "Huh?"

"My fish I mean."

"You named them Fred and Wilma?" He smiled, and it was so infectious I couldn't help but smile in return, and a tiny part of my fear lifted enough to let the sunshine break through the growing clouds in my head.

"I can't believe I never told you, but I like the *Flintstones*, and *Scooby Doo*, oh and *Tom and Jerry*. They're cool, and I'm a massive nerd."

"Says the man who's sleeping with the person who jumped him when he dressed as Thor." He smiled. We kissed. It was perfect. "Anyway, I already have Jed finding an expert to move them to my place. It's all good."

"Okay."

"Come live with me?"

"Can I pay rent?"

He laughed and hugged me tight. "Sure thing, Mr. Richie Rich."

. . .

I LASTED A COUPLE OF WEEKS, RIGHT UP UNTIL WE WERE three days out from filming on *The Cup*.

The furor had died down, everyone was right about that, but there was so much pain in the world, and bit by bit, it nibbled away at me. The kids who wrote and said I gave them hope, the parents who saw their kids in a new light, contrasting with the nutjobs who blamed me for anything that ever went wrong, including the weather, and hoped I died. I could take the hate, but being responsible for carrying the torch for queer kids and families was too much to bear, because how could Finn Kerrigan, soap star, lucky fucker, wannabe serious actor, be held up as a beacon of hope?

Moving in with Cam was perfect. We fit. Fred and Wilma arrived and had pride of place in Cam's kitchen —our kitchen, he kept saying—and waking in his arms every morning was bliss.

But out there, with filming, and the messages, and the hopes and fears, there was more than I could handle, and the complex emotions were a fizzing ball of worry that stole my creative thoughts. I didn't have a therapist, but Atlas hooked me up; only one session in and all I felt was that I was a fraud.

Who was I for people to look up to?

"Finn? Earth to Finn?"

I glanced left at Cam, bobbing next to me in his vast pool, the faint sounds of rock music echoing from the property next door, and a camel staring at us over the fence.

"Huh?"

"You were miles away."

"There's a camel." I pointed at the inquisitive animal, who huffed and turned to leave.

"Yep. But that isn't what's got you staring into the middle distance."

He floated us back to the side, into the shallower end, and we sat on the steps, the early evening sun warm on any exposed skin.

"What if I fuck everything up?"

"You're worrying about the movie? Don't. River says you have an eye for the script, and he's convinced it will be big."

"I don't mean the movie."

"Then what? Sweetheart? What?"

I leaned on him, every emotion bubbling to the surface, and my eyes filled with tears.

"What if I can't be the person that people want me to be?"

He held me when I cried like a confused, exhausted toddler, and I felt foolish and low and fucked-up, and still he held me.

We both heard the buzzing at the same time, and I glanced up, a drone hovering over the pool, way up high. I heard a bang, and the thing disintegrated, some of the pieces splashing into the deep end of the pool, one larger part slamming into the gazebo.

"Got it!" someone yelled next door.

"Fucking paps!" another voice yelled back.

"See!" I shouted at Cam, right in his face. "It's hurting your life now! We may as well end it before this destroys us. Fuck! I need to go." I knew I wasn't making sense, but the heartbreak in Cam's eyes turned to flinty determination.

He held my hand and tugged me up and out of the water.

"Fuck them and fuck this shit. We're going inside."

Chapter 18

Cameron

For some reason I was in full caveman mode.

Guess this was my Fred Flintstone era.

Whatever.

Tugging Finn behind me, I stormed into my house, slammed the doors, and called out to Alexa to close the horizontal blinds. As the room slowly darkened, I released Finn, turned, and tried to get him to a calmer place. It might have worked if I weren't as keyed up as I was. He was for sure feeding off my vibes.

"We're going to meditate," I told him. His eyes rounded. "Yeah, I said it. We're going to sit down, close our eyes, and find our center."

"Uhm… okay?"

We padded further into the living room, removed the cushions from the sofa, then plopped our asses on them. He sat with his back against the couch, I used the side of my recliner for a backrest. Legs folded into a lotus, we sat across from each other, his tremulous smile helping to ease the rabid urge to throttle all the press bubbling like a rancid stew inside me.

A moment or two passed.

"Now what?" Finn asked.

"Well, we close our eyes, breathe, and say ohm a lot." I knew jack and shit about meditation. My sister was the real expert, but she was out of town with a young man and had left a rather snippy message in the family chat to not disturb her unless someone had died or was on the cusp. I could call my neighbor. Rottie had some sort of ancient guru from Tibet—or maybe it was Tahoe Vista—who came to his place twice a week to lead him through some mindfulness stuff. Nah. I didn't really want to subject Finn to Rottie while Finn was so frantic. Rottie was a lot. Maybe after I talked Finn down off the ledge he was teetering on. We'd need a hand to slip out of my place undetected. I could do the meditation thing. It couldn't be too hard, right? Sit and breathe. I'd seen Kelly do it a thousand times. Cake.

"Okay, I can do that." The tension around his eyes and pretty mouth had lessened. That was a good start. I leaned in to kiss him just once. He sighed in pleasure as his eyes drifted shut.

I sat back. We needed to chill. Not fuck. Not that fucking didn't release tension and lower stress levels. Hmm. Maybe we *should* fuck...

He began deep breathing, in and out, and whispering something I couldn't quite make out.

Feeling like a hot dog at a hamburger convention, I tossed out a few ohms here and there, peeking at him getting right into the meditation thing. Within ten minutes, Finn had drifted off to sleep, his chin on his chest, full zonk-out mode. I pulled a soft Mexican blanket from the back of my recliner and draped it over him.

Then, easing out of the room, I walked into the kitchen to make some tea. Herbal probably. That was what Kelly would suggest. I opened a few cupboards and yep, there were several boxes of tea from when she had been here last. I filled my sister's brass kettle, put it on the stove, and turned the burner on. Then, I pulled out my phone and rang the wild man at the base of the canyon.

"Holy shit, Cammy, did you see that skeet shot Milton pulled off?!" Rottie shouted in my ear. "We were out back just doing some target practice when that mother-humping drone showed up. We rode up the canyon like two lone rangers of the metal wild. Oh fuck, that is an awesome song title."

"Rottie, hey, yeah, thanks for the hand on the drone. Listen, Finn is napping right now, but in say two or three hours, we're going to need a hand getting out of here. Can you provide a diversion to pull the press and the fans gathered at my gate away?"

"A diversion you say. Fuck yes! I am the motherfucking king of diversions and glory holes. That was actually the name of my last album."

"Wow, that's quite the title."

"Right? Totally sticks in your cranial pan. Tell you what…" I heard him talking to someone in the room with him. The other guy let loose a maniacal laugh that put me on edge. "Okay, two hours from now you will get a text from Milton—

"Who's Milton?" I had to ask.

"Oh, Milton is the dude who's teaching me how to incorporate couples massage with mixology."

Ah. Sure. "Oh, wow, sounds great."

"It is. So, in two hours you'll get a text from Milton. It will say 'Go now!'"

"Is that it?"

"Well, yeah. Did you want some sort of Jason Bourne cryptic message?"

"Maybe."

He sighed. "Okay, fine. Look for a secret agent man type of message from Milton Puffly."

"His last name is really Puffly?"

"Dude, don't name shame."

"I wasn't! I just… sorry. Tell Milton I'm sorry. Two hours. Text from Mr. Puffly." I *so* wanted to laugh at that last name, but I behaved. "Then, we go."

"That's the plan, man. Listen, I have a little place in the UK that you could crash in. Oh, and a chalet in Sweden, overlooking a lake. Very posh. Swedish people are so welcoming."

"No, thank you. I'm taking him home to my family for a while."

"Ah nice. Your folks are the best."

He hung up. I stared at my cell. When the hell had he ever met my parents?

I thought to call him back, but I had packing to do. After I brewed tea and had a cup to settle my rage. Finn was sound asleep on the floor when I walked his cup out to him. He'd slipped down to his side, taking the blanket with him, his head now on the cushion. The man was exhausted. He had some dark rings under his eyes. Neither of us had been sleeping all that well, but Finn was carrying so much anxiety. Placing the lemon and lavender tea on the coffee table, I tucked the throw under his scruffy chin, then jogged to my bedroom to pack. I threw clothes into a couple of Storm duffels; uncaring what items went into the bags. Since most of Finn's clothing was now here, I soon had his duffel full as well as mine. I showered, pulled on some old shorts and a white T-shirt, and shoved my feet into sandals. Then, I sent my mother a text to let her know we were coming.

She and Dad were thrilled. They'd been clucking like two worried chickens ever since Finn had come out. I'd contacted everyone to warn them and explained that my name was going to be connected to Finn's as we were dating. After the shock wore off—I mean it wasn't that stunning of an announcement was it?—they all got sappy and happy for us.

I'd hoped to bring him to Scottsdale in less trying times, but the world had pushed us into taking refuge in my parents' gated community. Hopefully, the media would be held at bay at the gate. We could relax for a few days more, let things die off, and pray some other star did something worse than be themself.

When I strolled into the living room with our bags, Finn was awake, sitting up, and sipping his tea.

"I think I meditated myself into a nap," he commented, one eyebrow rising as he gazed at our packed bags.

"You needed the rest. We're heading to Scottsdale as soon as the distraction down in the canyon begins."

"Oh. That's nice. Will your folks be mad at me for dragging you and them into this mess?"

I dropped the bags by the door leading to the garage, walked over, knelt, and took his beloved face between my hands.

"They are not mad. They cannot wait to meet you. Dad is a huge fan. Mom is already making her famous homemade chicken tamales. Kelly will probably jet home to meet you even though she's off being swept off her feet by some man we have yet to meet, and Lyle will show up with his bride-to-be and offer you tax advice. Which, while boring, is generally really sound advice. No one hates you or the situation. It's the world that's made this into a big thing, not you, so no more worrying. They will love you."

He smiled, a genuine one that warmed his gaze. I kissed him gently. My phone pinged in my back pocket.

"That's either Rottie or Kelly," I said, giving the tip of his nose one fast peck before reaching to pull my phone out. It was my sister saying that she was heading home now. "The guy she was with made a crude comment, so she dumped her cocktail over his head, told him to fuck all the way off, and is now at the airport in Kingston working on a flight home."

"Aww, that's the pits for her," Finn said into his mug of tea.

"Yeah, well, he was a dick. Better she finds out now than get involved with the pudding head, then discover he's a homophobe."

"True."

I typed out a *sorry babe* to my sister, then sent her a dozen hug emojis. Lyle joined in, then, asking why so many silly emojis were needed in a family thread. Kelly and I both sent him about forty middle fingers to flood the page. My mother added a big *LOL* to the discussion.

"This is what being in the Chavkin family will be like," I told Finn, showing him my phone so he could read the interactions. He chuckled. "Right, so they're all going to be there by the sounds of it." Another ping pulled me from Kelly and Lyle sniping at each other over emoji use. Milton Puffly—OMG that name—had texted. Two words.

ROCK ON!!

I glanced at Finn. "Guess the diversion is about to take place." We stood, he tossed his throw to the sofa, and we hightailed it to the garage, Finn bouncing on one big foot, then the other, to cram his massive feet into some old Nike sneakers.

The garage door was barely halfway up when we heard it. Heavy metal music, blaring from down the winding street. It was so loud you could feel it in your fillings.

"What the hell?" Finn asked while buckling himself into my Jeep. "Holy shit," he gasped as he held up his phone for me to see. I looked up from sliding the key into the ignition to see a post on Rottie's Instagram page that read—

FREE CONCERT AT MY HOUSE! PLAYING UNRELEASED SONGS FROM UPCOMING ALBUM! COME ONE, COME ALL, COME HARD!

"No shit," I whispered, trying to comprehend what that would bring to our quiet little canyon. Rock and roll fans, scores of them, metal heads out the ass. "What a genius!"

We crept to the gate. Not one news van or reporter was stationed on the other side. I got out of the Jeep, peeked up and down the street, then rushed to drive through the gates. As the metal barriers to my home swung shut, we witnessed the first wave of metal addicts arriving in cars, vans, trucks, and motorcycles. Some were on bikes, rollerblades, and skateboards. I glanced at Finn. We both yanked on some old caps and dark sunglasses. Then, we pulled into the street, leaving the impromptu rock concert behind. The cops were filing in on the heels of the first wave of fans. Snickering to myself as we slipped out unseen, I had to imagine that Rottie's agent—whoever that poor bastard was—would be up to his eyebrows in citations after this.

"We owe Rottie for that," I confessed to Finn when we swung free of the canyon to head in the direction of Arizona.

"Maybe we can name our first dog after him," Finn suggested, pulling off his hat to let the air blow through his golden hair.

"Only if it's a poodle," I replied, and he laughed. It was a joyous sound, free and light, something that I'd not heard since his press release. It filled me with such joy I laughed too.

"Or maybe my next fish?" His fish had moved in with us now, and they couldn't be moved for a long time, which made me happy because we'd always have a connection even if…

Nope. We were not ending.

Hell, we'd only just begun.

Every mile from LA we drove, catching a night in a no-tell motel halfway there, Finn loosened up more and more. By the time we arrived at that fancy gate with the formidable guard in Scottsdale, Finn was loose as a goose. Given a pass a while back, I drove through and into a neighborhood of palatial homes, towering palms, and glistening ponds on sprawling golf courses. Yes, there were two just in this neighborhood alone. Why? God only knows, and even he was confused.

"This is quite the neighborhood," Finn said as we cruised at the respectable speed of twenty-five through winding streets with names such as Pink Mesa Lane or Sand Song Avenue.

"Yeah, it's really something. Hard to imagine that my grandparents on my mother's side were migrant farm workers, and today, their daughter lives in a home like this. Goes to show that the American dream is alive and well," I replied as we pulled a left off Gold Valley Way up to my parents' modern adobe home. Finn whistled at the view of the mesa that lay beyond my family's fourteen acres of desert, sand, and geckos. Pinks, purples, and a dark blue like the color of Finn's eyes after making love colored the sky.

"This is amazing. I can feel the desert gods calling to me to come relax and be safe here," he whispered, enthralled with the sunset. "It's kind of magical."

"Yeah it is." I couldn't argue. Arizona was stunning. I was proud to be a native son. The front door burst open, and my mother ran down to the driveway. I got one peek at Finn's face before she embraced him. His blue eyes had been round as manhole covers.

Mom kissed his cheeks, patted his face, and then, hugged him once more. Dad stood in the doorway, snickering, as my mother led Finn inside without giving me a backward glance.

"Chopped liver," I sighed, gathered our duffels, and tromped into the house.

"She's over the moon to know that you finally found someone to settle down with," Dad confided as we hugged at the front door.

"Is she picking out names for the grandkids already?" I enquired. It was a legit question since she was already doing so for Lyle and Carmine.

"Not yet but give her a few minutes." Dad clapped my shoulder, took our bags, and nudged me toward the huge kitchen. "Grandma is back and waiting to see you. Don't mention the latest tattoo on Grandma's ankle. Your mother is not at all pleased."

"Grandma is the best," I whispered. Dad nodded, then went upstairs to drop our bags in one of the guest rooms.

I padded into the kitchen to find my grandmother seated at the island on one side of Finn, my mother sitting on the other, stuffing him full of chicken tamales and black beans on the side. "Hey now women, give the man room to breathe."

I slid in between Finn and my grandmother, pecking her wrinkled cheek as I moved into the small space.

"He's so handsome," Grandma said, then reached up to pat my cheek. "I got some new ink! Look!" She hiked up her pink legging to show me the butterfly on her ankle. Mom huffed. She was not a fan of tattoos.

"That's awesome," I replied, giving Finn a wink. He nodded, cheeks puffed with food, sapphire eyes sparkling in delight. Yeah, this had been the right thing to do for sure. "I'm thinking of getting a new one myself."

Mom rolled her eyes. Grandma clapped. My older brother, the party pooper, sauntered in through the back door with a glass of purple iced tea in one hand.

"You know that most businesses frown on hiring people with tattoos. They're seen to be tacky, low-class, and criminal," Lyle interjected. "Personally, I feel that they're fine for the lower classes, but—"

Grandma flipped Lyle the bird.

Finn spewed tamale all over the island.

My mom erupted into a litany of Spanish, chastising my grandmother. I nearly passed out from laughing, while Lyle sputtered under his breath.

"What did I miss?" Dad asked when he entered the kitchen a moment later.

"Grandma gave Lyle the finger," I managed to say between bouts of wild laughter.

"Mother Rosa," Dad teased, kissing her on the cheek before padding round the island to give my mother's hand a squeeze. Finn glanced at me, cheeks wet with mirth, his smile sweet and so sincere.

"You can back out now. This is the norm here at Casa Chavkin, and it will only get worse when Kelly arrives," I warned Finn while Grandma began dishing more beans onto his already overflowing plate.

"Nope, you're stuck with me. I love your family already."

"And I love you," I whispered beside his ear as I drew him into my side.

Mom beamed at me around Finn.

This whole relationship thing was okay. I should have tried it sooner, but then it wouldn't have been Finn. Maybe my heart was just waiting for the right person to come along so it could open fully. Just like the flowers atop many cactus that only open at night.

So that made Finn my moon and stars. No secret there.

Epilogue

Finn

"I can't believe I made it to this alive after all that falling over on the ice," I confided.

Cam laced his fingers with mine, and for a moment, I admired the man who was a million times sexy in his tuxedo, his eyes wide as we edged our way through the crowd to the drop-off zone. He wasn't the only one who was in awe of the sheer magnitude of people we'd passed, and I was glad I'd taken my meds, because my anxiety and inability to handle this would have killed me tonight.

"I'm not sure we will make it out of the car alive," he muttered and stared at the fans outside the tinted windows. The premiere of *The Cup* was tonight, and we were already running ten minutes late, which was entirely Cam's fault.

At least, that's my story, and I'm sticking to it.

He said the bathroom blow jobs were all my fault,

but how could I have known that me in a white shirt and purple boxers turned him on?

He said I should realize that everything about me turned him on.

I made a mental note to add half an hour to every appointment we had from now on, because I'd walk around in a dress shirt and boxers all day long.

"Five minutes," Jed called from next to the driver. It was reassuring that he was still with me, Todd having moved on to pastures new. Jed was now my official bodyguard, but in fact, I had a team of three who rotated in keeping an eye on me whenever I was away from the house.

I wish I could say it was to stop movie fans who wanted a bit too much of me, but it wasn't entirely about me being out in my career. Cam and I had received our fair share of hate concerning our relationship, and with the hockey season restarted, every loss was blamed on my influence somehow. Thankfully, wins outweighed their losses by a large margin, so at least that was something. I could handle that kind of baseless nonsense, but it was the more personal stuff, the threats themselves, that meant it would be some time until Jed would be leaving his role.

"It's carnage out there," Cam said, and slid along the seat to tug me close. "Think maybe we can stay in the car?"

"Says the big bad hockey player," I teased and got a

kiss for my words, which I'd been counting on. The kiss was a soft promise.

Bright lights shone in, as people tried in vain to get photos. We straightened ourselves as the limo drew to a stop. Jed was talking to someone, tapping his ear, looking all badass. "Two minutes," he instructed, then got out of the car. He would wait for a pre-determined moment to let us out, and then, it was time for the red-carpet walk. Reviews had been kind so far, and even though I doubted it was Oscar-worthy, I'd done my absolute best, pouring my heart into my character, so much that River had been talking to Atlas about two more movies he wanted to work with me on.

The *Rapid* franchise had just released movie four, with a brand-new lead, because there was nothing stopping that gravy train from rolling. Cam and I had snuck into the back of a theater to watch a week after release, and I'd enjoyed the hell out of the story, and was pleased for the new lead and the fact that they'd kept Luca Bennetto in his role. I was also secretly happy that the reviews were on par with the ones that had been written when I'd been the face of the franchise.

I hadn't stopped skating—that was something I did at least two or three times a week. I'd also gotten involved with Cam's kids' charity, sponsoring a couple of families—including Manuel's—in education and support for the arts. *Variety* called us a powerhouse couple, *TMZ* said we were cute, and the paps were pissed that there were too many photos flying around of Cam and me naked from the waist up. We'd done a photoshoot where we wore barely nothing, and since then, there'd been no more drones over Cam's house. The place we'd made our own.

It could have been the photoshoot, or the fact that Rottie kept shooting each drone out of the sky.

Not to mention the unfortunate incident with the camel and the pap who'd managed to get through Rottie's property and onto ours, which put the rest of the paparazzi off going near us. Cam's place was officially now our place—I'd bought fifty percent, which he promptly donated to charity, but still, I felt settled.

In love.

This was forever.

"Ready?" I asked Cam.

He winked at me. "Yep."

"And you remember what Atlas said?"

He counted off on his fingers. "No mauling you on the carpet, no being rude to people, no cursing, just walk with you and talk with you, and be a perfect gentleman. I really don't know what Atlas thinks I'm gonna do here."

I narrowed my eyes at him—he was giving off very strong vibes of being up to something.

I stepped out first, the roar of fans loud, invasive, and the best thing ever. I spotted rainbow flags in the crowd before camera flashes stole my vision completely. Cam was out right after me, holding out a hand, which I took.

Then, he swung me close.

Bent me back in a theatrical sweeping kiss and went to one knee holding out a box with two platinum rings.

"I love you. Marry me?" he asked. "And stay with me forever?"

What else could I say? I might have been tempted to remind him that Atlas would be pissed, but instead, I said yes.

And the rest of my life started right there, with a kiss on a red carpet, from the man I loved.

———

WANT TO READ A FREE BONUS SCENE FEATURING FINN & Cam's wedding at Christmas? Click here for the free short story - **Sparkle - details on the next page**

Sparkle

A Christmas Wedding Short Story

featuring Finn & Cam from Script (LA Storm, 1)

https://geni.us/lasparkle

Being in love with a Hollywood star isn't all it's cracked up to be. Neither is planning a secret holiday wedding to said box-office hero. There's the press and paparazzi to outfox, the wedding planner to please, and the catering to sort out. All of that while juggling a crushing hockey schedule and dealing with the world's most annoying neighbor. But despite the setbacks, worries, and flight plans for family, I've never been surer of anything in my life. Marrying Finn Kerrigan is everything.

https://geni.us/lasparkle

What's next for the LA Storm?

Second (LA Storm, 2)

Bryce has lost everything he loved. Michael is rebuilding a life built on lies. Is their love worth fighting for?

In the high-stakes world of professional hockey, Michael "Zeetoo" Zhang had the potential to shine brighter than his older brother. But he chose a treacherous path, and the scars of past failures and the constant shadow of his brother's success haunt him. After a run of bad luck, and angry at the world, his resentment intensifies when he's arrested, then sentenced to work supervised hours at an inner-city community garden. He's already lost hockey and his house; how can he afford to lose anything else?

Bryce Kincaid is chased by his own demons, and years after the mistakes he made, he's determined to never lose control again. He's built something stable and good from the wreckage of his life, and the last thing he needs is a pampered celebrity anywhere near his beloved community garden project. When Michael arrives, he's a broken man wrapped in a fiery package. But the gardens work their magic and reveal a vulnerability in Michael that Bryce can't resist, he's terrified to open his heart, and their growing relationship might be nipped in the bud.

To change his life, Michael must confront his past and fight for a future he never believed he deserved. But when that past threatens to destroy everything Bryce has built, their love could be over before it's begun.

Hockey Series' from RJ Scott & V.L. Locey

Harrisburg Railers

Owatonna U Hockey

Arizona Raptors

Boston Rebels

LA Storm

Chesterford Coyotes - Young Adult

Railers Legacy

Rochester Copperheads (AHL, coming soon)

Oxford Knights (coming 2027)

Railers Legacy

Speed (Railers Legacy 1)

Hard ice. Fast cars. Fierce love.

And a race against fate.

Hockey is as natural as breathing for Noah. Growing up with two famous hockey stars as his dads, Noah has always aspired to join the Railers to continue the Lyamin-Gunnarsson legacy. With his degree done, it's time to live that dream, and the first step is being drafted by the team his hall-of-fame dad played for. The second step is to pull on that dusky blue-gray sweater and make his fathers proud. His rookie year is bound to be a season of incredible highs and lows, but one of the biggest highlights is meeting Brody Vance at a fundraiser.

Brody is the living epitome of a bad boy hiding his pain behind a devil-may-care attitude. As Noah struggles to keep one eye on the puck and not on Brody, it's only a matter of time before both loves collide in a chaotic splash of media attention.

Bad boy racing driver Brody has spent his life chasing speed and glory and is only points away from his first world championship when a devastating crash ends his season. Determined to make a triumphant comeback, Brody is blindsided by a diagnosis that forces him off the track for good. With his world flipped upside down and family and fans questioning why he left, Brody hides his pain by pushing the limits and refusing to let anyone see the cracks. But after a chance meeting with a sweet, sexy hockey player turns into an unforgettable one-night stand, fate keeps putting Noah in his path. With his heart on the line and his body racing against time, Brody must decide if he's willing to risk it all for love—or if he'll let fear and pride leave him in the dust.

Speed is a steamy M/M romance with a hockey rookie living his family legacy, a bad-boy racing driver with secrets, media attention that would break even the strongest of men, an unforgettable one-night stand, a love that means risking it all, and a hard-won happily ever after.

Railers Legacy

1. *Speed*
2. *Blitz*
3. *Powder*
4. *Fly*

Harrisburg Railers

When hockey wunderkind Tennant Rowe meets his new coach, he knows he's in trouble. Jared Madsen is nine years older than Tennant, impossibly attractive, and — worst of all — his brother's off-limits best friend. Is their chemistry worth the risk?

Changing Lines (Railers 1)

Can Tennant show Jared that age is just a number, and that love is all that matters?

The Rowe Brothers are famous hockey hotshots, but as the youngest of the trio, Tennant has always had to play against his brothers' reputations. To get out of their shadows, and against their advice, he accepts a trade to the Harrisburg Railers, where he runs into Jared Madsen. Mads is an old family friend and his brother's one-time teammate. Mads is Tennant's new coach. And Mads is the sexiest thing he's ever laid eyes on.

Jared Madsen's hockey career was cut short by a fault in his heart, but coaching keeps him close to the game. When Ten is traded to the team, his carefully organized world is thrown into chaos. Nine years his junior and his best friend's brother, he knows Ten is strictly off-limits, but as soon as he sees Ten's moves, on and off the ice, he knows that his heart could get him into trouble again.

———

Harrisburg Railers (Hockey Romance)

1. Changing Lines
2. First Season
3. Deep Edge
4. Poke Check
5. Last Defense
6. Goal Line
7. Neutral Zone
8. Hat Trick
9. Save The Date
10. Baby Makes Three
11. Rivals
12. Perfect Gifts
13. Family First

Railers Volume 1 | Railers Volume 2 | Railers Volume 3 | Railers Volume 4

Owatonna U, College Hockey

Meet the men of Owatonna University's hockey team

Ryker (Owatonna U, 1)

Ryker is hockey royalty, Jacob is a poor country boy. Can two vastly different people find common ground and become the men they want to be?

Ryker comes from a long line of championship-winning hockey players. Playing college hockey to develop his game is his only focus, and nothing will stand in the way of him working to become the best player. He has no room for relationships, people who point out his flaws, or anyone who calls him on his dreams. He certainly has no place for love, and meeting Jacob is nothing but a useful distraction on the side. After all trying to get his Owatonna Eagles teammate into bed is less work and more play. When tragedy rocks his family, his charmed life crumbles, and the only person he can turn to is the same one who claims to hate him.

Jacob Benson has only known hard work and stifling conservative values his whole life. Born and raised in the small rural community of Eden Crossing, Minnesota, he's the only son of a hard-working but struggling dairy farming family. Jacob is using his skills in hockey to finance his way to an agricultural science degree. These four years at Owatonna U. will probably be the only time he has to enjoy life, gain acceptance about his sexuality, and live openly before his inevitable return to the farm. Running into a pretty rich boy like Ryker Madsen is putting a damper on his enjoyment of life away from home. Ryker's flip, conceited, carefree attitude grates on Jacob's every nerve. So why, if Ryker is everything he dislikes, does he want nothing more than to explore the sinful dreams that his annoying teammate stars in every night?

Ryker

Owatonna U Hockey (Hockey Romance)

Arizona Raptors

Coast to Coast (Arizona Raptors 1)

Coast To Coast

When opposites attract, this bottom-of-the-league team will never be the same again.

A stipulation in his father's will forces Mark back into the arms of a family that disowned him and leaves him one-third owner of a hockey team facing financial ruin. He doesn't even watch hockey, let alone like it, and wants nothing more than to head back to New York. Then there's the new coach, a stubborn, opinionated, irritating man with superiority issues and questionable music taste. Butting heads with Rowen becomes the new normal, but it comes with passionate debate and an all-consuming lust.

Challenged to rebuild one of the worst teams in the league into a future cup contender, Rowen can't pass up the opportunity. Never in his twenty years of hockey has he ever seen a team managed so badly or coached players overflowing with resentment and bigotry. Yet there's something about this team and this city that compels him to roll up his sleeves and start dismantling. If only Mark, one of three siblings who now own the Raptors, wasn't so damned rock-headed yet so damned appealing his job might be easier. It doesn't look like either is willing to give in, but one night in a dark, desert hotel changes everything.

Coast To Coast

Arizona Raptors (Hockey Romance)

1. Coast To Coast
2. Across the Pond
3. Shadow and Light
4. Sugar and Ice
5. School and Rock

Boston Rebels

Top Shelf (Boston Rebels 1)

Acting on the attraction to his best friend's brother has always been off the table for Xander until a passionate hookup with Mason at a beach resort begins a love affair that burns long after summer ends.

Mason specializes in assisting same-sex couples on their journey to becoming parents and fighting every rule that blocks his way in the stuck-in-the-past agency that hired him. Living in his brother's pool house is rent-free, and every cent he earns he saves for his dream—that one day he'd have his own company helping others. The downside is that he has to see his annoying brother every day, the upside is that his brother's teammates from the Boston Rebels make regular visits. The eye candy that passes Mason's window is almost enough to make him consider dating a hockey player, but not just any player though. Ever since Xander—his brother's childhood friend—came out as gay at a press conference, Mason's puppy love has turned into a burning attraction he can no longer ignore.

Hockey has been one of Xander's main focuses since he was old enough to balance on skates. Well, hockey and Mason Kingsley, but Mason was always unattainable. Now that he's about to see thirty candles on his birthday cake and is no longer hiding the fact he's gay, he's ready to find a soul mate to make his life complete. A summer vacation is just what he needs to have time to think, but when the Boston Rebels arriving in paradise with Mason in tow, thinking is the last thing he needs. One torrid night under a balmy moon and rules about not messing with his best friend's brother vanish on a warm, tropical breeze.

Summer romances don't generally last past Labor Day, but with the new season about to begin Xander and Mason are going to have to face the world and decide if their love is real enough to withstand everything.

Boston Rebels

Lost In Boston (Free Prequel Novella)

1. Top Shelf

Chesterford Coyotes, Young Adult Romance

Off The Ice (Chesterford Coyotes, 1)

Off The Ice

A coming-of-age love story with high school, hockey rivalry, friendship, family, and coming out.

Soren's life changes in an instant when he and his younger brother are adopted by hockey royalty. Making sense of his new life is hard enough, but when he's enrolled in a private school it means facing a whole new set of problems. Navigating friendship, family, and hockey is one thing, but being attracted to the boy who vexes him is a whole new thing.

Felix has a reputation to protect. He's the kid who seems to have everything but looks can be deceiving. Spinning lies about his perfect life, he's created a fantasy world that even he has started to believe. Only, it's not long before everything crumbles, all of his pretty lies are revealed, and only his closest rival sees through his pain and stands by him.

Fighting is easy, friendship is hard, but love is everything.

Off The Ice

Chesterford Coyotes

Free Reads

Please note - in all of these free stories, there will be some spoilers for the main series books.

Railers Short Stories

Volume 1 | Volume 2

LA Storm

Sparkle

The Colts - AHL Short Stories

Pucks & Percentages

Breakaway

Making the Save

Standalone

Waiting for Christmas

Also By RJ Scott

For a full list of ebooks and links please scan the code above
or visit rjscott.co.uk/rjbooks

Meet RJ Scott

RJ writes MM romance—sometimes sweet, sometimes dark, always with a generous splash of angst and a hint of hurt/comfort.

A born romantic, she's convinced love is love—and every man deserves his happily ever after (especially the ones who swear they don't).

Website - gayromance.co.uk
Newsletter - gayromance.co.uk/mailing-list

Scan for a complete list of ebooks and links.

instagram.com/rjscott_author
amazon.com/author/rj-scott
bookbub.com/authors/rj-scott

Also By VL Locey

For a full list of ebooks and links please scan the code above
or visit vllocey.com/stories-from-vl-locey

Meet V.L. Locey

V.L. Locey loves worn jeans, yoga, belly laughs, walking, reading and writing lusty tales, Greek mythology, the New York Rangers, comic books, and coffee. (Not necessarily in that order.)

She shares her life with her husband, her daughter, one dog, two cats, a flock of assorted domestic fowl, and two Jersey steers.

When not writing spicy romances, she enjoys spending her day with her menagerie in the rolling hills of Pennsylvania with a cup of fresh java in hand.

vllocey.com | vicki@vllocey.com
Newsletter - vllocey.com/newsletter

Scan for a complete list of ebooks and links.

facebook.com/V.L.Locey

x.com/vllocey

instagram.com/vl_locey

bookbub.com/authors/v-l-locey

goodreads.com/vllocey

pinterest.com/vllocey